I0780159

Memoirs of a Servicycle Gypsy

My Life on the Road

By Cherie Coon

ISBN 979-8-9904131-0-8

Published by Cherie Coon

Prolog

My younger family members have encouraged me to write the memories I have of the travels of my family in the late 1940's. I was very young at the time. I had just turned two when the journey began. That said this memoir is made up not only of my remembrances but of the tales told by my other travelers over the years. Many of them are my own since this time had such an impact on me. I have a distinct advantage in writing this as I am the last one alive to have made this journey. As such no one can contradict my story. Therefore, you will have to take my word for it that this is exactly how it happened. Whether it is all true or not, it is a good story. It is my story.

Well, I guess the first thing I need to do is explain what a Servicycle is. After all, if you have no clue what that is, this book won't make much sense. Of course, it may not make much sense, anyway, since I am now in my, so called, "Golden Years" and I'm going to tell you about my preschool years. Golden Years. If you ask me, that is just a nice way of saying "older than dirt". But I am wandering here.

Let's get back to where I was before I got sidetracked. What is a servicycle? I am pretty sure that you, dear reader, have at one time or another seen a World War II movie. One of the old black and white films where the Americans were all handsome and honorable and the German's all looked either like Col. Klink or Tab Hunter. The Tab Hunter look-a-likes were the ones trying to rescue the Jewish children hiding in the attic before the Col. Klinks could find them. The American GIs always got there in time to save the day whisking the kids to safety. Now, I'm pretty sure, you know what movies I am thinking of. Next step is to picture those motorcycles the soldiers zipped around on throwing up the mud as they roared through quaint villages and bombed out towns. These motorcycles I'm talking about are the ones that are about half-way between a wimpy moped and a manly Harley Hog. That, my friend, is a Servicycle. Remember how the handsome, virile American GIs would use them to rush ahead and outsmart the evil Hun by turning the road signs the wrong way? Or how they tore back through the enemy lines to let the bumbling Captain Ordinary know the front line was in deep doodoo and reinforcements were needed, like yesterday? Yep, that's the wonderous mode of transportation I am talking about.

Now on with my story.

Chapter One
Pre-Me

I guess this story really begins several years before I made my grand entrance. Let's start with my mother. She was a lovely young woman who had grown up in the small Ohio village of Laurelville. She was your iconic hometown sweetheart. The May Queen. The captain of the girls' basketball team. Ingrid Bergen look-a-like. I think you get the picture.

After she graduated from Laurelville High, previously known as Toad Run Academy, my mother left her small town in southeastern Ohio to attend nurse's training in Columbus at Grant Hospital. World War Two was roaring through Europe and the need for trained nurses was sure to be an issue soon. Shortly after Pearl Harbor, as she was finishing up her training, one of her fellow nursing students introduced Mother to her brother, John. Three months later Daddy had won Mother's heart, and they were married. They only had a few weeks together before Daddy was on his way to Alaska where he was to work as a civilian aircraft mechanic. Since the war was heating up it was several months before the paperwork came through and Mother was able to join him. For a small-town girl who had never been more than 100 miles from home, it turned out to be quite a journey.

My grandfather drove her from Laurelville to Union Station in Columbus. After a tearful goodbye she started on her big adventure. The first part of her trip was a train ride from Columbus, Ohio, all the way across the country to Seattle, Washington. When she arrived in Seattle, she was put on a list to take a troop transport to Alaska. She and another wife, who was also on her way to Alaska to join her husband, had to wait several weeks until space for them became available. While in Seattle, Mother and Juanita became good friends and enjoyed being two young women on their own in a strange city. Seattle was very different from Ohio. The scenery, the strange people and food, and of course the weather. Finally, two berths opened on a ship heading up the Inside Passage, the safest way to Alaska, and they were on their way.

The first leg of their journey ended when the ship let them off in Skagway. At that time, Skagway was a small village on a fiord where the float planes could land. The plan was to fly them from Skagway overland to Anchorage. All went well for a half hour or so, then the plane's engine started acting up. They had to make an emergency landing near a tiny Native American village. Mother and Juanita were housed with a family in the village while they waited a week for the parts needed to fix the plane to arrive. For two girls from Ohio this was a new experience.

Finally, the parts got there. The crew got the plane running again and the pilot took it up for a test flight. He took it up but didn't bring it back. He crashed into a mountain shortly after taking off. As Mother and Juanita recovered from the shock, they waited for another plane to come to pick them up and finish the trip.

After a long, scary trip they finally arrived at Ft. Richardson in Anchorage. It had been several months since Mother had kissed her new husband goodbye. When she stepped onto the tarmac there was a group of men waiting to see if their wives were among the passengers. Much to Mother's chagrin, she didn't recognize Daddy. Luckily, he recognized her.

When she first arrived, they lived in a small rental house Daddy had found near the post. They were only there a short time as Daddy had found a shell of a house he could buy. He started finishing it when he was off duty. He was able to scavenge enough from the packing material on post that in a few months he was able to make the house livable. This house was located out at the edge of town with a good view of the mountains.

While Daddy worked on aircraft at Ft. Richardson, Mother got a nursing post at the big hospital downtown. She was considered essential personnel since the hospital was the one the military also used. In order to be sure, she got into the hospital for her shift each day, the Army issued her a vehicle.

But not just any vehicle like a jeep or a pick-up. Nope, what they issued her was a deuce and a half. Yep, my beautiful, Ingrid Bergman look-a-like Mother drove one of those big troop hauling trucks. Each morning, she climbed into the driver's seat and started her drive into town. Along the way, she would pick up any soldiers needing a ride to the Fort. After dropping them off she would proceed to the hospital. Then at the end of the day, she would swing by the Fort, collect any men waiting along the road and drop them off on her way home.

My parents had a wild time in Alaska. And I mean that literally. Moose hunting, fishing for salmon and all the outdoorsy things that one associates with Alaska- they did them all. Mother even tried her hand at panning for gold. She never found any but she had fun.

One of Mother's favorite stories was how she, Daddy, and several of his buddies from Ft. Richardson went moose hunting. They hiked two days into the back country and set up camp. So, of course, that meant it was a two day hike out. They camped on a bank above a swift flowing river which was in spring flood. I'm not sure if they managed to kill a moose, but it must have been quite an experience. Daddy's buddies were kinda' on the nervous side about Mother going with them, though. They were really far out in the wilds. Daddy was totally cool with it. He saw no reason a woman eight months pregnant couldn't go moose hunting. Yep, you read right. She was eight months pregnant with her first child. As most of you know babies sometimes come early. Daddy's attitude was that she was a nurse and knew what to do if the baby decided to come a little early. Besides, women have been having babies on their own forever, haven't they? Luckily, the baby held off until they got back to Anchorage.

Three weeks later, at the end of June, my brother, Kent made his entry into this story. Kent spent his first six months in Alaska. At the end of Daddy's contract, my family packed up and headed back to the lower forty-eight.

Mother, Daddy, and Kent in front of their house in

Daddy carrying water from the well to the house.

Mother going ice fishing.

Mother with Dougie Unwin on the sled. Daddy holding their dog, Totem.

Daddy hanging out diapers.

Chapter Two

The Wild West

Their first stop along the way back to Ohio was Seattle. Daddy considered taking a job with Boeing and even got a job offer from Pan Am. But they both missed family. They also had that baby boy, born in Alaska, who needed to be introduced to his relatives. Plus, a carrot had been dangled in front of Daddy- an offer of a partnership in my great uncle's auto dealership in my mother's hometown. They spent almost a year in Seattle enjoying the beauty of the Pacific Northwest. When the war ended, they decided it was time to head back to Ohio. So, they bought a house trailer, hooked it to their car, and headed toward San Diego. Yes, I know, that is not the way to Ohio from Seattle. The thing is, my uncle Frank was getting mustered out of the navy there. So, the plan was to drive down the Coast and pick him up before heading east.

They packed up their trailer, said their goodbyes to the friends they had made in Seattle and jumped on Highway 99 south. They crossed the mighty Columbia River, wound their way through the Willamette Valley, and started the climb over the ridge of mountains in Southern Oregon. They struggled over the Siskyiyou Range into northern California as the day was ending. On the southern slopes they pulled off to camp for the night.

The next day they decided to take a break and catch up on some domestic chores since there was a clear stream bubbling over the rocks nearby. While Daddy built a fire to heat water Mother pulled the water tub out of the trailer. Daddy rigged a clothesline as Mother carried a few buckets of water from the stream. Soon she had a nice warm tub of soapy water to wash Kent's diapers. By midmorning she had a line full of nice clean diapers drying in the breeze.

As they headed south, they passed the snow-capped volcanic peak of Mt. Shasta. For miles they watched as the regal beauty slowly rose over the rolling plain. As the highway looped around it, they saw a sign for Mt Lassen National Park. Since they were not in a hurry, they took a detour to visit the park. After touring Lassen, they continued south stopping to see any interesting sights until eventually they came to San Francisco.

Mother fell in love with San Francisco. She was charmed by the cable cars and the houses perched on the hillsides. The majesty of the Golden Gate bridge as it reflected the sunset awed her. Fisherman's Wharf was a delight. Her highlight was getting to eat abalone.

Ever one for adventure, after they got passed San Francisco, Daddy decided to drive down route 101, the Pacific

Coast Highway. There was only one little, tiny problem with this plan. There had been a landslide, and the highway wasn't open to traffic. Did that stop Daddy? Heck no, those barriers were easy to move. They made it but I have been told I came very close to not happening since there were times the car and trailer were rubbing against the side of the cliff as the seaside edge was adding debris to the beach below. But they did make it, and so here I am.

They stopped to see Beverly Hills, Hollywood and all the sights as they passed through LA. They took the Celebrity's Homes Tour to see where all the glamorous and rich movie stars lived. They picked oranges right off the tree. They walked down Rodeo Drive to see all the expensive glittering stores. They checked out the stars on the sidewalk in front of Grauman's Chinese Theater. Then with stars in their eyes they continued their southward trek.

They reached the port in San Diego in time to see Uncle Frank's ship come in. A weathered seaman in Navy whites mustered out and duffel bag in hand joined the caravan. After a short time of enjoying the beach, the seafood, and the warm climate, they headed east.

They began a leisurely, winding trip across the West. Their path led them to all the major sights, especially the National Parks. Leaving San Diego, they headed northwest. They marveled at the Joshua trees. In Quartzite they stopped to pay their respects to Hi Jolly, the camel driver of the US

Calvary. What? You don't know about Hi Jolly? How is that possible? Then let me enlighten you. During the Indian Wars of the late 1800's an Arab Prince gifted the US with a couple dozen camels. The southwest, where the Indian Wars were being fought, was desert so what better transportation then a camel? And to help the US troops learn how to manage the camels the prince sent a camel driver with them. The American troops had difficultly pronouncing the driver's name. The best they could do was Hi Jolly. So, Hi Jolly he was for his time in America. He stayed with the camels long after the experiment had ended. When he died, he was buried in a small cemetery in Quartzite, Arizona. The monument to him stands there to this day.

From Quartzite they followed the Colorado River north to where Hoover Dam was nearly finished. From there they drove east to the Grand Canyon before turning north to the National Parks of Utah. After visiting Zion, Bryce, and Arches, they crossed the Rockies into Colorado. Once they reached the Great Plains, they got serious about the trip and headed at a steady pace eastward. After this long and winding journey they finally arrived back in Ohio.

Mother and Kent on the porch in Seattle

Daddy and Uncle Frank at Hi Jolly Memorial, Quartzite, AZ

Spot on the journey near the Oregon/California Border where they stopped to do laundry

Chapter Three
Enter Stage Right

When they finally reached Laurelville, if they had had them back then, Mother would have needed one of those Baby on Board signs. My big debut was in the not-too-distant future!

Once they settled into life in Laurelville, Daddy was all set to take over Uncle Bill dealership. To make a long story short, that carrot was not forthcoming. Yantie had exaggerated. The idea was for Daddy to be a mechanic for Uncle Bill garage when they needed one. That would not provide enough work to support our family. Daddy took over the Shell station at the edge of town instead. Mother and Daddy had opted for a country life, renting a house a couple of miles out of town. Once they were settled in, it didn't take long for me to show up.

For some reason, they decided I would make my appearance at Grant Hospital in Columbus. That was probably because Mother had done her nurses training there. When it looked like it was time, Mother and Daddy hopped in the car and started out on the fifty-mile drive to the hospital. (Yantie, my great-great aunt, was at the house to stay with Kent.) As they were on the drive Daddy noticed some nice fat ground hogs in a field along the road. Since Mother's contractions were still not too close together, he decided to stop and see if he could get one. After all a nice young ground hog is fine eating. In short, he didn't get a ground hog and they made it to the hospital before I put in my appearance. Actually, they made it to the hospital in plenty of time. I was in no hurry to leave the nice warm place I had inhabited for the previous nine months. While Mother was trying to persuade me to come forth, the doctor told Daddy he had plenty of time and he might as well get something to eat and take in a movie or something. Yes, you guessed it. He had only been gone a short while when I decided enough was enough and made my debut.

Back home in Laurelville after my arrival, we settled down to good old country living. The house we lived in was a couple miles out of town. Mother had her chickens and a young milk cow. Daddy had his own business. Kent and I had family nearby to spoil us. The garden provided all the vegetables we could eat. Sound like a perfect life? Mother thought so.

For two years things seemed to be going well. But Daddy was a Spencer so after a couple years his feet started itching. About that time Uncle Frank showed up again and threw a monkey wrench into the whole shebang. And it was one heck of a monkey wrench. When the war had ended a couple of years earlier the U.S Army found itself with thousands of these servicycles with no one to ride them. The soldiers had been mustered out and were home with their families. They were building houses, having babies, going to college. Just generally getting on with their lives. So, all these servicycles were added to the millions of dollars of army surplus that was now available for sale –Cheap! Uncle Frank had found a hundred or so servicycles in pieces packed in barrels of grease and bought them for a song. No, he didn't really sing to get them, he had to pay money but from what I gathered not a lot. It didn't take very much of an argument to convince Daddy that we should head south in search of adventure and riches selling these fantastic (cheap) bikes. And that is just what we did eventually.

Kent on the porch where we lived near Laurelville, Ohio

Daddy holding me at the Shell Station in Laurelville, Ohio

Chapter Four
I'm Florida Bound

By late 1948 we found ourselves living in a house trailer behind my Uncle Jim's house in Dayton, Ohio. Daddy was from there and his brothers all lived nearby. Bear in mind that the "house" trailers back then were like today's small camping trailers. Ours was 8 feet by 16 feet and that included the trailer hitch. While Kent and I bonded with our cousins -Kent learning to make tomato can bombs from his older boy cousins and me having fun splashing in the all the mud puddles left from the recent construction of Uncle Jim's house- Daddy and Uncle Frank planned this big adventure. One of the first things they did was to buy a wrecked school bus. After pounding out the dents and overhauling the engine, they removed what was left of the banged-up seats and painted it battleship grey. Now that color was not chosen because they particularly liked the color but because there was still a lot of paint of that shade left in the US Navy Surplus stores. And again, it was very cheap. The driver's seat of the bus was mangled in the crash so they figured they might as well get rid of it, too. Across the front of the bus, they put a beat-up old couch which doubled as a driver's seat and a place for Uncle Frank to sleep on this journey to adventures and riches. The empty back of the bus they filled with barrels full of servicycle parts, tools and our few belongings that did not fit in our luxurious house trailer, which was most of them.

So, in early November we hooked the trailer to a rusty pickup truck and with Frank driving the bus and Daddy driving the truck, we headed south. Now November was not the best time of year to head south on the two-lane highways of the late 1940's. Especially in a vehicle that had old tires and with no spare, but those feet were itching so off we went. Mother was not so much into this big adventure as she was very much a home body. She would have been more than happy staying right there in Laurelville, feeding her chickens, milking her cow, and planting a nice big garden. But off we went anyway. The plan was to head southeast from Dayton and stop for a goodbye visit in Laurelville, then we would be on our way for real. Mother had already taken Kent and me to our grandparents in Columbus and said her goodbyes there. We had an early Thanksgiving with the rest of the family in Laurelville before heading out for real. The day after the big feast, loaded down with turkey dinner leftovers, we were on our way. Just before we crossed the Ohio River into Kentucky, Daddy stopped and filled the two propane tanks that sat on the trailer hitch at the front of the trailer. We would be using propane for the small furnace by the door of the trailer and to cook with. For light we had a Coleman lantern. Many nights I fell asleep to the gentle hiss of the flame.

Things were going pretty smoothly until we crossed the Ohio River into Kentucky. There we were greeted by the local constabulary. He said he was "right happy" to know we were just passing through his beautiful state but in order to do that we needed to have license plates on the trailer. Alright, so we missed a minor detail. Picky, picky. You can't think of everything when you're off in search of adventure and riches, now can you? He was nice enough to escort us to the local department of motor vehicles located in the county courthouse. He also gave Daddy a hand-written note. I think he called it a ticket.

While Daddy and Frank visited with the nice people in an office in the courthouse, Mother read to us in the lobby. Have you ever noticed that there is a certain smell found in the hallways of small county courthouses in the Midwest? It's almost as if the perfume is leaking out of the marble in the floors and columns. They all smell alike, I've found.

Soon Daddy and Frank emerged from the office, and we headed to where we had left our gypsy caravan. Daddy put the license plate on the back of the trailer while Mother got Kent and I settled in the truck. All loaded, and legal, we were soon on our way again! And only a little bit lighter in ready cash. As the day was ending, Daddy started looking for a place we could pull off and camp for the night. It wasn't long before we found a pullout along a small river and set up camp. Mother lifted her wash tub of house plants out by the side of the trailer so we could get inside. As soon as we climbed in Daddy set the tub back in to one side of the door and squeezed his way through. Mother lit the stove and soon had a supper of hot home-made vegetable soup bubbling on the stove. When we had visited my grandparents, Grandpa had given us a dozen or so quarts of his great vegetable soup, thick with chunks of beef from the steers he raised and vegetables from his huge garden. Add some bread and butter and you have a feast. Or so we kids thought. Uncle Frank was of a different mind. He was more of a steak and taters man. An assessment he often voiced as our journey continued.

The next morning, we continued slowly but surely southward. That is until the morning of the third day. That's when we had our first flat tire. And, since we had no spare there was only one thing to do. Take the tire off and hitchhike to town to get it patched. Now you may ask why didn't Daddy and Uncle Frank just drive the bus into town rather than hitch hiking? Did I mention we were very short on cash? Even more so after our little visit with the nice people at the Ohio/Kentucky border. So rather than use up gas to drive to a town and back, why not use someone else's gas and hitchhike. Town of course was quite a way off and Mother knew it would take hours, so we headed back to the trailer. To pass the time, we baked Christmas cookies. To this day the smell of a propane stove makes me think of cookies, we baked tons of them on this trip. It was getting late when the men finally made it back to the caravan so Daddy decided we should just spend the night right there where we were.

From then on this was our pattern. Every couple of days Daddy and Uncle Frank hitched to town while Mother, Kent and I baked cookies. We soon had the most patched up tires in the country but an ample supply of Christmas cookies.

Then we hit the mountains. Not only were our tires in bad shape but we very quickly discovered a pinpoint hole at the top of the radiator. As we started chugging up the first of the mountains, steam started rising in a fine mist from the front of the truck. Luckily, we were just about a half mile from a town that had a store. So, we limped in with a wispy cloud hoovering over the front grill of the truck. Now I know you are thinking that we would have stopped in that town, asked around and found a local mechanic who had the know-how to repair our leaky radiator. Once said mechanical genius was located, he would fix the wayward radiator. But you forget, we are Spencers. And if there is one thing that can be said about Spencers, it's we NEVER do things the normal way. And besides, the radiator wasn't a problem when we weren't in the mountains. And the mountains only kept going up for a few days. So instead of a repair man, Daddy ran into the grocery and returned with a big bag of penny bubblegum. Tossing a couple pieces to each of us he ordered us to chew like crazy. As soon as one of us had a nice mushy wad worked up, Daddy pulled over and jumped out of the truck. He ran to the front where he could reach the offending radiator and stuck the wad of gum over the hole. By the time he got back to the truck whoever had provided the gum would have been given the next batch to start working on. Off we would go for twenty miles or so until the wad of gum had melted off and steam started to appear again. The next chewer would hand over their wad of gum. And so it went until we were over the mountains and rolling down toward the flats of southern Georgia.

Somewhere just north of Atlanta while we were still in the hill country, we encountered one of the most interesting characters I would ever run into in my long life. Coming up the road toward us was the Goatman. This gentleman was a legend. Not only could you hear him coming but if the wind was coming from the right direction, you could also smell him. Or I should say you could smell his goats. He was slowly making his way along the side of the road in a rickety cart attached to a half dozen goats of varying sizes. Riding on the cart was a bearded, long-haired man dressed in tatters. The cart was loaded with all kinds of stuff, pots and pans hung from the sides and banged against it as they moved along. Running along the side and to the back of the cart were more goats ranging in size from old bucks to young kids. Many of the goats had bells hanging around their necks adding to the din. We stopped our caravan and waited for him to get close. By the time he reached us we were all lined up along the road to greet him. He stopped and visited with us for a few minutes before bidding us goodbye and continuing on his way.

An interesting note. Years later when we were traveling down a much-improved highway with a more reliable vehicle, we again encountered the Goatman. His beard was a little grayer and his cart a lot more ramschackled, but it was the same man we had meet on our journey to Florida in the late '40s.

There was one flat tire stop that was particularly memorable for me. It was somewhere in the hills of northern Georgia where the soil was that deep rich red that you associate with this area. We were parked on the side of the road miles from any town. We could see a weathered house, not much more than a shack, a little way down a dirt road leading off the highway.

By now we were far enough south that the temperatures were nippy but not really cold, so Mother had aired out the trailer a bit and was sitting on the door sill while Kent and I played. There were wild vines with small wild gourds on them covering the ditch that ran along the edge of the road. Kent and I were having fun picking the gourds and playing catch. We would throw one back and forth until someone dropped it and it exploded. Okay, until I dropped it, but I did catch some of them. Then we would hunt among the vines until we found another. After an hour or so we tired of our game, and besides evening was coming on. We had joined Mother by the trailer and were trying to talk her into reading to us when a young boy and little girl walked up the lane from the house. They both wore well-worn rubber work boots. The boy had on patched overalls and a plaid shirt. The little girl was wearing a flour sack dress that had seen better days. Shyly approaching us, the boy said, "Ma'am, Ma said I was to come up here and fetch you and the young'uns down to the house afore it got full dark."

Mother, ever polite, replied, "That's very nice of your mother but I wouldn't want to be any bother."

Rubbing the toe of his boot through the red dirt and looking at the ground, he explained, "Well, ma'am, Ma said iffen I came back without you she'd snatch me bald headed, so I'd be obliged iffen you'd came with me.

Now how could anyone refuse that kind of invitation? Asking them to wait a minute, Mother gave my face and hands a quick wash. They were filthy as usual since I was a world class dirt magnet. Then scratching out a quick note to Daddy and grabbing a tin of cookies, we followed the children down the dirt lane.

By the time we neared the house it was almost dark. The coal oil lamps inside gave off a soft glow through the windows. Opening the door for us the boy invited us inside. We were greeted by the smell of popcorn filling a warm cozy room. The mother greeted us with a friendly smile and led us toward a table where they had been stringing popcorn and cranberries to hang on the tree. Mother and Kent followed her into the kitchen area of the room, but I never made it to the table. Over in one corner of that room was the most beautiful, most glorious, most wonderful thing I had ever seen. It was a spindly pine tree stuck in a coffee can of sand. But it had lights all over it! And not just ANY lights. No sirree. These lights had moving BUBBLES in them! And they were all different colors! Yeah, and there were tin foil stars and other stuff on that tree, but those lights were awesome! Finally, Mother noticed me standing there with my mouth hanging open and quietly told me I could look but not touch. In my awed state I could only nod. After standing mesmerized for a while, I dropped to the floor and stared at those lights until I must have dropped off to sleep on the floor because I don't remember anything else. I would dream of those marvelous lights for many years to come.

The next day, Kent told me, not without a hint of disgust, that I had embarrassed him by just staring at their Christmas tree like dope. And I had not helped to string the popcorn which was probably a good thing since I probably couldn't do it anyway. None of which bothered me in the least. But I was a little miffed when he told me how many cookies he had been allowed to eat. I didn't really care too much about the cookies because the important thing was, I got to see that wonderful tree. I don't remember how I got back to the trailer. I guess when Daddy got there to collect us, he had carried me back to the trailer because when I woke up the next morning, I was in my bed in the trailer.

For the next few days, I couldn't forget about that beautiful tree. While I daydreamed about the tree, Kent kept talking about Christmas. I kinda' got that it had something to do with presents and that tree was important to those presents but I just didn't get it. Since I was only two and a little more, I really couldn't remember Christmas the year before. But Kent seemed to be obsessed with it. I might have asked Kent more about it but since he seemed so worried that this year it wouldn't happen, for once I kept my mouth shut.

Several days later after we had passed Atlanta, we were in the flat part of the state passing through lots of fields filled with dried plants that had wisps of cotton sticking to them. Kent was getting more and more nervous about this Christmas thing the farther we got from Ohio. Near lunch time, we had stopped in a small town for gas and a rest break when Daddy told us he had a big surprise for us. As a special treat we were going to eat at a restaurant. It seemed like it was Uncle Frank's idea since right after we had stopped, he had gone into a restaurant to buy a pack of cigarettes. When he came out, he had pulled Daddy to one side for a confab. He always talked with his hands a lot and he was pointing to a building up the block from where we were stopped, then to the restaurant and back to that building. Whatever they were discussing Daddy seemed to think it was a good idea. When he and Uncle Frank had finished their chat, Daddy came back to the bus where we were waiting. After winking at Mother, he told us about lunch in the restaurant. Mother was thrilled as this meant she didn't have to cook a big meal when we stopped for the night and could get by with sandwiches. I just hoped they had hot roast beef sandwiches with mashed potatoes and gravy.

We all trooped into the restaurant. Except for Uncle Frank, who seemed to have something more important on his mind than food. This was very strange since if there was one thing Uncle Frank liked it was food. As we enter the restaurant the waitress said we could sit wherever we liked so we settled around a table covered with a red checker tablecloth. They even brought me a booster seat so I could see the table. And hallelujah, they had hot roast beef sandwiches with mashed potatoes and gravy. After we ordered Mother took me into their bathroom and gave me a good scrub so I would be reasonably clean when the food arrived. As we waited for the food, Daddy kept commenting on the songs playing on the radio on the shelf behind the counter for some reason. It was okay music but not what we usually listened to on Mother's record player. Uncle Frank came in the door just as our food came and gave Daddy a thumbs up. Then he ordered a hamburger from the waitress and sat down at the counter with a big grin on his face. We had just gotten started on our food when the music on the radio was interrupted for a special announcement. Daddy shushed us and told us to listen. He said it might be important. So, we all hushed up and turned our attention to what the man was saying. Over the radio we heard-

Attention! Attention! I have a special announcement for Dooley County, Georgia. This special announcement is for Kent and Cherie Spencer traveling somewhere in Dooley County.

Did our ears ever perk up at that! We looked back and forth between Mother and Daddy not knowing what to think. I mean we were Kent and Cherie Spencer. And we were in Dooley County, Georgia! That must be us they were talking about! The announcement continued.

This is a special message from a Mr. S. Claus. I assume that would be the one and only Santa Claus. Anyway, here is his message for Kent and Cherie Spencer. "Don't worry. Santa knows the whereabouts of each and every good boy and girl in the world. I will be sure to visit you on Christmas Eve. No matter where you are, I will find you." And now back to our regularly scheduled broadcast.

Kent's eyes looked like saucers and he had a grin that stretched from ear to ear. I still didn't quite get it but figured it must be something pretty good or he wouldn't be so happy. And this Santa person even thought it important enough to put a message on the radio. And to think we were lucky enough to be where we could hear it. If we had been traveling, we would have been out of luck because we didn't have a radio in the truck. After a wonderful lunch of hot roast beef sandwich and mashed potatoes and gravy, we were ready to hit the road again.

There were some days in the afternoon Daddy had driven the bus and Uncle Frank drove the truck. Daddy said it was to break the monotony. I may have been young, but I had figured it out. It was so I could take a nap on the felt mat they had put over some of the barrels behind the couch. After our lunch stop that day Daddy, Mother, Kent, and I headed for the bus as Frank climbed into the truck. I crawled back to my nap place as soon as we got on board and snuggled down for a nice snooze. With Mother and a very happy Kent on the couch beside Daddy, we headed south again.

Late one afternoon when I was awake from my nap and was playing on the mat, we stopped in a small town not far from the Florida border. There was a fruit stand under the trees in the town square where we had parked. Uncle Frank had made a beeline for it when we pulled in and now, he was walking back toward us with his ungainly walk. He was carrying something bright orange and seemed really pleased with himself. He handed one to Mother and Kent then as I watched he took the skin off this small orange fruit and pulling it apart he handed me one of the pieces. "Here, Florida Girl, this is like eating sunshine!" I popped it in my mouth and a burst of juicy goodness exploded in my mouth. That was the first time I remembered eating a tangerine. And it was the best! I decided I just might like this Florida place.

The next day we started seeing long strings of Spanish moss hanging from the trees. Daddy said it meant we were getting close to Florida which sounded good since I was getting tired of riding every day. By midmorning we had crossed the state line out of Georgia and were officially in the Sunshine State. Not sure why it was called that because right after we crossed the state line it started to rain. Oh boy did it rain. The road filled up with big puddles and when there was a low spot it was almost like driving through a creek. We crept along slowly. By late afternoon, we finally arrived in a small town not far from the state line. Just as we pulled into a gas station, the rain turned to a soft drizzle. We were in Lake City, and this turned out to be the first stop on our journey to riches and adventure. We all piled out for a good stretch despite the rain. Daddy and Uncle Frank went inside to ask the owner if he knew of a vacant lot, we could rent to set up the bikes. Daddy explained we would be making a dirt track but that was the only thing we would change on the lot. After some thinking and consulting with the old guys hanging out there around the Coca Cola cooler, they decided on a place to point us toward. Before nightfall, we were parked on a vacant lot on the east side of town not far from the railroad tracks. While Daddy and Uncle Frank unhooked the trailer and leveled it, Mother fixed a quick supper. Once we ate it was time for bed. Kent and I slept on the twin beds in the back of the trailer. Mother and Daddy bunked down on the hide-a-bed in the front. The layout of the trailer was as follows- A bedroom that was two twin beds side by side against the wall and a narrow passage between. There were drawers under the beds for storage and a tiny, mirrored vanity against the back wall. The rest of the trailer was a kitchen, living room, dining room combination. The kitchen had a stove that burned propane, a sink (which didn't have running water) and a small built-in refrigerator but it only kept things cold if you put a block of ice in it. The dining room was a table that you slid in to collapse. When it was pulled out you could barely walk around. There were four folding chairs that crowded around the table and a highchair for me. The living room, which was four steps from kitchen, held the couch which made into the bed where my parents slept. I'm not sure what Mother, Daddy and Uncle Frank did after we went to bed, but they were still busily working when I dozed off.

When I woke up the next day Daddy and Uncle Frank had already put together one servicycle and were working on a second. It took a couple of days to assemble a dozen bikes and make the dirt track. The track was the biggest job they had to do in the setup. Uncle Frank used a heavy rope to tie an old railroad tie he had found down by the tracks to the back of the truck. He had wrapped a chain around and around the tie before he hooked it to the back bumper of the truck. Dragging this round and round in an oval, he leveled and dug up the ground until he had a well-defined dirt track. Now we were ready for business. And it was a good thing since the young men of Lake City were chomping at the bit to try out these cool new toys.

Left to right- Daddy, Uncle Frank, and Uncle Jim. Kent in the foreground. Planning the trip.

Uncle Frank on one of the servicycles

The bikes in front of the bus.

Chapter Five
Life in the Sunshine State

The next morning, we were open for business. They put up a sign that said, "Five laps for a Quarter." Mother had her first aid kit out and ready for all casualties. Now all we needed were a few customers. We didn't have long to wait. For a couple months, the young guys in the area showed up every day to rent one of the bikes, riding it around and around the dirt track. Then after weeks of riding in circles, they started talking about taking one out on the road. Daddy told them the only way to do that was if they bought one. He set a price for them. They talked him down a few dollars. He told them that was rock bottom. They headed off to see if they could raise the money.

"So how much did you settle on?" asked Uncle Frank when they left.

"How does $25 sound to you?" replied Daddy, chuckling.

"Now that sounds mighty fine. I thought we were going to try to sell them for $20."

"I started at $35 and let them talk me down to $25. They think they got quite a deal. Put one over on 'that Yankee fellow'," replied Daddy laughing.

Then a few weeks later two of them showed up wanting to buy the bike. They had raised the $25 and with cash in hand could hardly wait to obtain this great toy. Daddy went over all the things they should know about the maintenance and safety of the bike. They listened impatiently and when Daddy finally finished, two spankin' new bikers happily rode off into the sunset on their cool new machines. It was nice to see the young men so happy. But the best part was Mother had money to go to the grocery store!

While we were in Lake City, I learned all about this Christmas thing Kent had talked about all the way from Ohio. A week or so after we were all set up, Daddy came to the trailer with a little pine tree. Mother and Kent were really excited about it, but I just saw a scraggly pine tree. Daddy filled an empty coffee can he had picked up from behind the local diner with sand and set it next to the front door under the awning. While he was getting it set up, Mother pulled a box out of the storage space under the bed. In the box was a string of bright shiny stuff that we wrapped around the tree. Then there were some glass balls and stars and stuff. And even some lights! They were not the marvelous BUBBLE lights that were on that other tree, but these were almost as pretty. They were a lovely shade of blue. Then we hung long strands of silver icicles all over it. Daddy had talked the people who lived next to our lot into letting him run an extension cord so we could plug in our Christmas tree. They were nice folks so they said we could. When Daddy plugged in the lights it was beautiful. The blue lights reflected off the icicles and made the whole tree glow. I decided our tree was just fine even if the lights did not BUBBLE. We sat out under the awning at the side of the trailer and looked at our tree as the sun set and the light faded. It was even more beautiful when it got dark. But soon it was bedtime, and besides the mosquitoes had come out so for now the lights were turned off and we headed inside.

A couple mornings later, Kent woke me up early because he said Santa had come during the night. I looked around for this Santa guy, but it was just us. The first thing I noticed was the socks we had hung up the night before had bulges in them like something had been stuffed inside. We spent a while looking at what Santa had put in our socks while Mother got breakfast. Kent kept insisting I call it my "stocking", but it was just a plan old everyday sock. Nonetheless, I was pretty happy about all the goodies in it no matter what it was called. We each got a candy cane, two tangerines and new panties. Well, I got panties, Kent got underwear. By then Mother had breakfast fixed and we all sat down to eat. Kent was having a hard time sitting still during breakfast. He kept looking at the door as if something super special was out there. Once we had eaten most of our breakfast,

Mother said we could go out to see if Santa left anything under the tree. Kent popped up from the table like a jack-in-the-box and made a bee line for the door. As soon as he opened it, we noticed the stuff under the Christmas tree. There were a bunch of boxes all wrapped up in shiny paper and tied with ribbons. It turned out these were the presents Kent had been talking about all the way from Ohio. He was so excited I figured I should be excited, too. We tumbled out the door and he started picking up the paper wrapped boxes and asking Daddy to read the label on them. It seemed everyone had at least one package under the tree. Kent got a real authentic Roy Rogers six shooter cap gun and holster set. As soon as he unwrapped it, he strapped it around his waist. It made him look like a real cowboy. All he needed was a cowboy hat and horse. When I unwrapped my present, it turned out to be a big baby doll. Once I had my doll, I lost interest in Kent's present because all he wanted me to do was to watch as he kept practicing pulling his guns out and saying bang your dead. After all it gets boring when your part of the game is just to fall down and lay still. So, I wandered off and I spent the rest of the morning bonding with my new friend, Pinkie. We got some other presents, too. But they weren't as exciting. We both got new tee shirts and pajamas and some other clothes, but my new doll, Pinkie, was the best! I decided I liked Christmas a lot. The only bad thing about it is you have to wait a whole year for it to happen again. A year is a very long time to wait when you're little.

While we were in Lake City I met my very best friends. They stayed with me the whole time we were in Florida. Nobody else seemed to be able to see them but whenever I went out to play there they were. Orangie and Diane. They really liked Pinkie. We could play for hours. Dressing Pinkie. Feeding Pinkie. Taking her for walks. I never got lonely as long as I had my friends. And the best part was, they understood everything I said. You see, I had a problem with certain sounds. For instance, I couldn't say my S sounds and F's and TH's and… I think you get the picture.

About this time the old rusty truck disappeared, and a real car showed up at our camp site. It had no rust and even better a backseat! Now we could all get in one vehicle and go on day trips. And boy, were they fun! One day we drove over to Jacksonville and went to the beach. I liked it there a lot! I could dig in the sand, chase the sea gulls and I never imagined there could be so much water. It didn't stand still very good though and kept knocking me down. Also, it tasted awful! But we all had fun swimming, fishing, and looking for seashells.

Another time we went to a place near the Georgia border that Kent said was a National Park. Mother called it Okefenokee Swamp, but Uncle Frank called it the Boolly Woolly Wamps. I liked his name the best. It was a strange park because they didn't have any swings or slides or seesaws, just a lot of dark murky water, trees with roots sticking up like knobby knees and all kinds of other plants. They did have lots of turtles, birds, and big scary alligators though. So, it was pretty fun looking for the animals.

The other place I really liked was a place called Ichetucknee Springs. It was a crystal-clear pool with a white sandy bottom. There was a spring in the middle where the water bubbled up to feed a stream that ran from it through the swamp to empty into the Suwannee River. The water was really, really cold but it felt wonderful on a hot day. We would go there for a picnic and then play in the water all afternoon. The other people there told us to be sure to leave before it got dark because the wild pigs come down to drink as soon as the sun went down. Those pigs didn't sound very nice, so we made sure we left before sunset. We went there several times while we were living in Lake City. One of the best times was when we took a bunch of inner tubes and floated down the river. The river was clear with waving bright green grass and little silvery fish darting here and there. But on both sides of the river was swampy brush so once you started you had to go all the way to the bridge where the road crossed the river. After a couple of hours, we came to the pull-out point where we paddled to the shore and got out. Uncle Frank had driven the car down here when we got in the water, and he was waiting to help us out of the river. We were all tired and a little sunburned. By the time we got back to Lake City all I wanted to do was go to bed.

All was well for us there in Lake City for several months, then one afternoon the county sheriff showed up for a visit. It seemed one of the guys that bought a bike from Daddy had wrecked it and was in the hospital. The sheriff said he would take kindly to us moving on to a new location. Preferably, across the county line. He would stop back in two days to see if we needed any help moving on. Daddy assured him we could manage by ourselves and thanked him for the offer. So, we started packing.

Chapter Six
Movin' on

The next day we were on the road by noon. As we moved along toward the south, we stopped at a couple other places down the road to see if we could find a place to set up, but it seemed like their sheriff knew the sheriff in Lake City, so we kept driving until we got to Palatka. We had trouble finding a place at first. Uncle Frank asked at a couple of gas stations but each time we were told there was nothing in town we could rent. We were on our way out of town when we finally found a spot we could rent by the railroad tracks, again. Mother seemed concerned that we were on the wrong side of the tracks. Both sides looked just the same to me, so I was a little confused.

Soon we were settled in and renting out the bikes again. I had figured out about the wrong side of the tracks by then. The kids on the other side were a different color than Kent and me. When we saw them, we waved at them, and they waved back but they didn't seem to want to play with us. They seemed really nice though. One day Kent coaxed one little boy close enough to talk to by showing him his Roy Rogers six shooter cap guns. He looked at them from a short distance away. When Kent asked him if he wanted to play, he said he was not allowed. His mother had told him he had to stay away from "that riffraff down the road". I guess we were riffraff, whatever that was. So, we went back to the trailer and played by ourselves on the big green rug under the awning.

Even though they wouldn't play with us I liked being close to where they lived. On some nights whole families used to sit out on their porches and sing. There was one song I liked a lot. It was a song the men sang when it was just them sitting out after the women had taken the kids home to put them to bed. They would be out there singing as I was trying to get to sleep. The song was about a girl named Irene and they were telling her good night. It was so nice and soothing the way their deep voices blended together. The window in the trailer would be open, the bugs would be flying against the screen trying to get to the light. Then softly in the distance, these lovely deep voices floated through the air and into my bedroom. It was the thing I liked best about Palatka.

I was very relieved when we got there to discover that my two best friends were there, too. The first day when I went out to play there were Orangie and Diane. After that as soon as I got up and dressed, I would go out under the awning with Pinkie and Orangie and Dianne and play. Some days they had red hair, other days yellow hair like mine. One day Dianne even had green hair. Kent said I was just being stupid again and they weren't really there but Mother said he was to let me play and not tease me. We had lots of fun playing together under that big yellow, green, and orange striped awning. Since they were always there, I was never lonely.

One day we went to a place called Silver Springs. We had left Uncle Frank to take care of the bikes so we could take our time. We even brought the trailer so we could have a little vacation. Saying it was a vacation seemed funny to me because it was just like being at home since the trailer was home. Sometimes I just didn't understand adults. But anyway, Silver Springs was like Ichetucknee Springs only a lot bigger. They had boats with glass bottoms so when you rode in them you could see all the pretty fish. There were paths that wound between the huge live oak trees draped with Spanish moss. There were also concrete walkways that ran along the water so you could look down into it at the fish and waving grass. The grass was a vivid green against the silver white sandy bottom just like it had been on the river flowing out of Ichetucknee Springs. We were all walking along on one of these walkways looking at the fish and grass and birds when I heard a splash. I looked around trying to see where a fish had jumped to make that splash. I was puzzled because there were none of the usual rings left when a fish jumps. I turned around to ask Kent about it when I noticed Kent was not beside me anymore. I looked back up the path, but he had not wandered off in that direction. He liked to climb trees but after checking all the trees he might be able to climb I didn't see him in any of them. Then I heard another splash and a gurgle. That's when I thought to look in the water next to the walkway we were on. Yep, there he was in the water, sputtering and splashing and looking very unhappy. He had walked right off the walkway and straight into the springs. I ran and caught up to Daddy and grabbed his hand. Tugging on it, I pointed to where Kent was struggling away in the cold water. Laughing, Daddy hurried back to where Kent was. When he got there, he reached down and pulled him out. Luckily, the day was warm so Mother moved him over to a bench in the sun so he would dry off. Kent was not at all happy about his unplanned swim. Since it was a really warm day, I thought a dip in that cold water would feel pretty good. I sat there beside him for a while just trying to decide how much trouble I would get in if I "fell" in, too. As tempting as it sounded, I was not sure anyone would notice in time to pull me out. Since I couldn't swim, I decided to pass on it.

Near where we were sitting was one of the glass bottom boats that had sunk. It was partly underwater, but you could still go inside. When you went down the steps into it you could see the whole pool through windows in its side. Daddy checked it out then came back saying he had a great idea. He called over his shoulder, "I'll be back. Wait there for me." Leaving us there on the bench, he jogged off toward the parking lot.

Mother yelled after him, "Johnny, where are you going?"

He yelled back, "I'm going back to the trailer for the movie camera."

"Bring a towel or two," Mother yelled after him. He gave her a thumbs up as he disappeared around a big live oak tree.

A few minutes later Daddy was back with the camera and two towels. Kent took one of the towels and began to dry off. The next thing we knew Daddy handed the camera to Mother and pulled his shirt off and stripped off his pants. There he stood in his swimming suit. He told Mother to go into the boat and film him. Then he walked over to the water and dove in. Not knowing what else to do Mother headed to the boat to film Daddy swimming in the Springs. Curious, I followed along and there was Daddy swimming just on the other side of the window. He swam around and around playing with all those pretty fish. Kent's curiosity soon got the better of him and he soon joined us in the boat. We stood with our noses pressed against the windows as we watched. Daddy continued to swim with the fish for a while then he started to get cold and swam over to the walkway and pulled himself up on to the edge. Kent handed him a dry towel. He dried off as best he could and pulled his pants and shirt on over his damp swim trunks. It was a good thing too since he had just gotten his clothes on when a worker came walking down the trail. He took one look at a shivering Kent and wet Daddy and wanted to know what the heck was going on. Daddy didn't exactly lie but it wasn't quite the truth either.

Smiling a big friendly smile Daddy said, "Well you see, sir, my son here was not watching where he was going, and he walked right off the edge into water. He can't swim so I had to jump in and save him. Now, if you will excuse us, I really need to get him back to our trailer so I can get him into dry clothes." And with that we all scurried off down the path toward the exit. I really don't think the worker believed us because he yelled after us, "Hey! Where'd you get those towels if the kid just fell in?" But by the time he had a chance to think it through we were long gone. As soon as we got to the parking lot we climbed in the car and moved down the road a few miles before pulling over so Kent and Daddy could get into dry clothes. After that Mother and Daddy decided we had had enough excitement for one vacation, so we headed home.

This is also about the time Daddy bought the orange utility trailer. We hooked it behind the bus to carry extra stuff when we traveled. And when we were settled someplace it became our camper. We liked to hook it to the car and load lots of stuff like blankets, pillows, my nap mat, food, and bathing suits into it and drive over to the ocean. One of our favorite beaches was Coco Beach. Once at the coast, we would find a place we could pull down onto the sand and set up camp. It was a great place to camp. Kent and I loved to play in the ocean near the shore. The best part was when Daddy would take first Kent then me out into the deeper water to ride the waves. When we were tired of that we would build sandcastles. Mother took us on long walks down the beach and we found lots of pretty shells that the waves had washed up onto the beach. Later as it got dark, Kent and Daddy would gather up some driftwood and build a big fire. Once it had burned down some, we roasted hotdogs and toasted marshmallows for our supper. The night sky was full of millions of stars. There seemed to be so many more at the beach than anywhere else. I would lay on the mat, listen to the crash of the waves, and look at the stars until I would finally drift off to sleep. You can really sleep soundly on a beach. The sound of the waves breaking on the sand is like a lullaby. The soft breeze rustling the sea oats on the dunes made a soft whispering sound. It was usually so peaceful there.

But one night we had a big scare. I was sleeping like a rock when all of a sudden Mother was grabbing me up and trying to grab as much as she could as she tried to drag me and the stuff up toward the dunes. I was so sound asleep I kept trying to lay back down which was not helping things one little bit. Daddy had pulled Kent up telling him to run but he was standing like a tree staring down the beach. That's when I came awake enough to see what was going on. I heard a loud roar and saw two very bright lights closing in on us- FAST. They were coming too fast to get out of their way, so Mother and Daddy threw us down and fell over us. Since the military used this beach as a runaway sometimes, Daddy kept saying, "It's an airplane. It's got to be. I just hope they get airborne in time." We huddled there in fear. The lights were almost on top of us, and the "plane" didn't seem to be gaining elevation at all. The sand was flying around us. We were sure this was to end.

That's when the lights started moving apart and two motorcycles roared past, one on either side of us. As they faded into the distance, we heard the riders laughing hysterically. It took a long time for us to all settle down and get back to sleep that night, I can tell you that.

The next day Daddy and Mother went fishing in the surf while Kent and I played. By the time the tide had changed, Mother had caught three nice big fish. Daddy cleaned them and put them on the ice in the ice chest and we began to pack up and head back to our camp by the bikes.

Camping on Coco Beach

a

Chapter Seven
And Movin' on Again

After Palatka we moved on. Again, at the request of the local sheriff. It seems they thought that it was Daddy's fault when the men who bought the bikes wrecked them. It didn't make sense to me but there you have it. What choice did we have? We packed up and moved on. This time to a place called Eloise. It was in what they called the Lake Area. There were lakes everywhere. I would have really liked to play in the water of those lakes except every time I thought one looked inviting, I saw alligators' eyes peeking out at me. That convinced me I should look elsewhere for a swim.

While we were in Eloise, Kent turned five. One of the most exciting things that happened there was the package Daddy picked up at the post office in town. Grandma had sent it general delivery which means she addressed it to the post office and people like us could go in, show identification, and get their mail. Since it was addressed to Kent, he got to open it. In the package was a very special present for him. Grandma had sent him a big new book. It was called "Song of the South" and was about all these talking animals. There was also a little boy and girl and a nice old man who told them stories. Mother must have read the four story books we had about a zillion times by then, so I was more excited about the book than the two new feed sack sundresses Yantie had made me even though they were my favorite colors, blue and purple. As soon as dinner was over and we had eaten some of Kent's birthday cake, we curled up on the couch and Mother read us the first story in our new book. It was about this fox, and this bear, and this rabbit. The fox wanted to do all kinds of awful things to the rabbit. Skin him. Roast him. And lots of other things. Each time the rabbit said that it was just fine and dandy with him, only he said, "Don't fling me in that briar patch!" I could see why he would not want to be thrown into a briar patch since my few run-ons with briars were not pleasant experiences but the other thing Ol' Brer Fox and Brer Bear (Mother explained that Brer meant brother) wanted to do to him were just as bad and maybe worse. Finally, Brer Fox decided to do what the rabbit asked him not to do. He grabbed ol' Brer Rabbit by the ears, swung him around a few times and flung him way up high and into the middle of the briar patch. Boy, was that old fox surprised when he heard Brer Rabbit laughing and singing "Born and bred in the briar patch". I couldn't wait to hear the next story, but it was time for bed, so we had to wait until later.

Eloise was a nice place. It didn't even seem to have a railroad track for us to get on the wrong side of. But, after a few months there, we were again invited to move on by the sheriff. Another kid had wrecked the bike he bought from us. I never was sure why it was our fault that these guys couldn't drive their new bikes without wrecking, but I guess it was our fault, so we packed up again. This time we moved to Plant City.

Kent and I playing in the water. One of our favorite things to do.

Chapter Eight
Fire!

In Plant City we found a place in a shady area not far from a big factory. Turned out it was a juice processing factory. You could tell each day what they were processing by the overpowering smell of the fruits and vegetables. Since they were processing all day every day, the smell had me hungry all the time we lived there. I was always looking for something I could get my hands on to carry off and gobble down. This is when I discovered I really liked oleo margarine. Butter was expensive, at least too expensive for our budget, so we had oleo as a substitute. My appetite for it began because I liked to watch Mother mix in the color. Back then when you bought oleo, it was this glob of almost white greasy stuff. It came with a little packet of bright yellow liquid that you mixed into the white stuff. It got all swirly at first then slowly the whole tub turned this warm beautiful yellow. When Mother was done, she used to give me the spoon to lick. From her reaction I think she did it as a joke the first time thinking I wouldn't like it. But I thought it was absolutely delicious. Soon I was sneaking into the ice chest and scooping out a fingerful from time to time. I got away with it for a few weeks then one day I got greedy. I took the whole tub out back of the trailer and had a feast. When Mother found me, I had practically polished it off. I really enjoyed it while I was pigging out, but boy, did I have a tummy ache that night! And the next day I had to go to the bathroom a lot, too. After that Mother usually managed to hide the oleo from me. She wouldn't have really needed to since I must admit, I wasn't so keen to eat a whole tub after that.

One of the most frightening things of our adventure happened right there in Plant City. Actually, it was way more than frightening; it was downright terrifying. I woke up late one night to a weird flickering light and people yelling. Mother was trying to wrap me in a blanket while handing one to Kent. She had just stepped out of the trailer as Daddy was throwing stuff in the trunk of our car when another car drove up and parked against the trailer hitch. I could sense Mother's panic. She was watching the flames shooting high into the sky from the juice factory and shouting about the huge oil storage tanks next to it. Between the roar of the fire and the loud popping sound of cans exploding, it made it hard to hear yourself think. Daddy approached the man who had blocked the trailer hitch and nicely asked him to move his car so we could get away from the fire. This man used some not too nice words and told Daddy he was here to get photographs of the fire and didn't have time to move his car. Daddy asked him again not so nicely this time while blocking his way. He again refused. Daddy asked him somewhat nicely one more time. When he again refused Daddy grabbed the man by the collar and dragged him back to his car. I have never seen Daddy so mad! He opened the man's car door and pushed him in. All the while, he was yelling at the man to move his car or he would take the wrench he had in his hand and either go after the windows of his car or, maybe, the man himself. Now I was really scared. I'd never seen my Daddy this mad. It worked though. The man moved his car and Daddy hooked up our trailer as quickly as he could while Mother, Kent and I scrambled into our car. We just barely got out of there before the road was so packed with people none of the traffic could move. We could hear the fire trucks in the distance but there were so many cars they couldn't get through to put out the fire. I climbed up onto the seat so I could see out the back window. The last thing I saw as we pulled away were flames shooting high into the sky.

It turns out Uncle Frank had seen the fire first and woke Daddy. He loaded the few bikes we hadn't sold into the back of the bus and headed out thinking Daddy would be right behind as soon as he hooked up the trailer. We caught up with Uncle Frank at the edge of town and pulled off there for the rest of the night. In the morning Daddy decided we could stay here for a few days while he and Uncle Frank went back to the dirt track to see if they could find any of the things we had left behind. That morning Daddy and Uncle Frank drove back over to our old campsite. They hooked the orange trail to the car and loaded it with anything we left behind. While loading up they notice lots of cans of juice and fruit scattered around the remains of the factory. Just before dawn, the fire trucks had finally made it through. By then the flames had died down enough to be on the safe side the firemen had hosed everything down cooling it off. Daddy looked at Uncle Frank then shrugged. Daddy picked up one of the tall juice cans and using his pocketknife opened it and took a drink. It tasted just fine even though it was still a little warm. So, they began to toss cans into the back of the orange trailer. After about an hour they were sooty and grimy, but the orange trailer was heaped with cans of juice and fruit.

When they got to where we were waiting with the caravan Mother didn't know what to think. The men were a mess and so were all the cans.

"You can't keep going looking like that," said Mother. "We need to find a place you can shower, and I can wash your clothes."

Daddy looked down at himself and laughed, "I guess you're right. Didn't we pass a trailer park last night on our way here? Maybe they'll have a spot we can park in."

That night we pulled into a real trailer park and after we got set up, the men headed for the shower house. Mother filled her wash tub and began cleaning up the cans. When she had them washed, she stacked them neatly into the orange trailer to dry. What we picked up kept us in juice for years. The only problem was, there were no labels. The fire had burned off the labels. Every time we opened a can it was a surprise. We had grapefruit sections, grapefruit juice, orange juice, mixed fruit juice, and my favorite- Bunny Rabbit Carrot Juice. There was also tomato juice, but I didn't like drinking that one. I have to say though, it was sure good when Mother put it in chili soup.

We stayed two nights at the trailer park so Mother could clean everything up and since they had a washing machine, she washed all our clothes, the bed sheets and everything else she could find that might need washing. It was a lot easier than using the washboard and the tub. There was also a big, long clothesline so she could hang all the stuff to dry at once.

Chapter Nine
Airplanes, Meteors and Fishing

Once again, we moved to a new location. This time our journey took us to Tampa. The only lot Daddy could find for the bikes was in an area where Mother refused to live. She also had had it with carrying water for cooking and laundry and giving us spit baths. This time we moved into a real trailer park. It had a swing set for the kids to play on, a bathhouse and a washing machine. One of the wonderful things about being in a trailer park was we could hook up to electricity and water. Nearly every other place we had set up we had no electricity and Mother had to carry water. The park was pretty. There were trees for shade. And best of all- other kids. Since it was not far from MacDill Air Force Base most of the families in the trailer park were military families. It didn't take long for Kent and me to get started exploring and the next thing we knew we were a part of the play group. We played cowboys and Indians, hide and seek, and even sometimes baseball although we didn't really have enough for two full teams. It was a great place for us kids. We had airplanes to watch flying in and out of the air base. There was an open field next to us that was a "forest" of palmettos. We could explore that and go on "safari". Kent always took his cap gun to make sure I was safe. After all he was the big brother, and it was his job to keep me safe. Orangie and Dianne were still around but they really didn't like my new friends all that much, so I didn't see them as often as I did when there were no kids around to play with.

On one of our excursions into the lot next to us, Kent and I were following a path into the palmettos when we heard an ominous thumping sound. *"Thump, thump, thump"* What could that be? Slowly, we eased forward looking left and right. Then we stopped and listened again. There it was again. *"Thump, thump, thump."* I could tell Kent was getting nervous as he had his cap guns out and cocked. Stepping in front of me, he whispered. "We have to be really quiet. And move really slow. Don't be afraid, though. I've got my guns, so I'll protect you." We listened again. *"THUMP, THUMP, THUMP"* Inching closer to me, he said, "That thumping sound must be the rattlesnake king calling his subjects to him. When he wants to make announcements to the Snake Kingdom, he beats his tail on the ground. That's how he calls them. Watch where you step because all the snakes in his kingdom will be showing up soon."

Now I didn't like the sound of that one little bit. Snakes were about my least favorite animal. Taking hold of his arm, I whispered, "Let's go home".

"No, I want to see the rattlesnake king and all his subjects. You can go back if you want but I'm going to stay here and see what happens. Go on back if you're a scaredy cat," he said rather haughtily.

Go back alone? Me? When there might be a rattle snake king around. Not to mention all the other snakes in his kingdom. Not on your life! I was sticking to Kent like glue. So, we cautiously crept forward jumping every time the breeze moved a leaf or branch. A few feet in front of us we noticed a small game trail cutting across the main path we were on. We neared this game trail one tiny step at a time. We stopped and looked both ways with each step. Kent was in front, and I was as close behind him as I could get without climbing up his back. Step. Shuffling step. Almost there. We eased forward by half steps. Almost there. Shuffle forward a few inches. *"THUMP, THUMP, THUMP."* We heard the sound off to one side only much louder this time. Shuffle forward a couple more inches. Suddenly, a large rabbit exploded out of the game trail and darted across our path inches from our feet. We both jumped and squealed.

Remember how Kent said he was going to protect me? I think he forgot that part because he almost knocked me over getting ahead of me to run back toward home. I stood there a minute watching the rabbit disappear down the game trail then turned and followed a rapidly disappearing Kent back down the path toward home. When I was almost out of the palmettos, I met Kent cautiously inching back up the trail to meet me. When I was almost to him, I ran up and hugged him. Then I smiled up and said, "Wasn't that a cute bunny?" He just took my hand and rather grumpily said, "Let's go home."

It seems that snakes were to appear more than once in my life while we were living in Florida. After the rattle snake king encounter that wasn't, we met up with a real snake right in the trailer park. I was on my way to the swing set with Pinkie one afternoon when I noticed all the kids gathered around a tree over by the bathhouse. Since I am always curious- okay, some would say nosy- I hurried over to see what was happening. As I walked around the tree to see what all the excitement was about, I came nose to nose with a hog nosed snake crawling up the side of the tree. In case you don't know, a hog-nosed snake has an interesting way of scaring off danger. It puffs up the skin around its head and flattens it out. Kind of like what a cobra does. It makes it look really threatening. It didn't take long for me to decide I had seen enough of that guy and I hightailed it back to the trailer. When I got there, Mother said if I left it alone it would leave me alone. But I noticed she went looking for one of the fathers in the park. He caught the snake and took it across the road and let it go. I just hoped it would stay there. After all this excitement Pinkie and I decided it would be more fun to play under the awning for the rest of the day. And anyway, Orangie and Diane had shown up. Best of all there were no snakes under the awning.

Since Mother and Daddy both liked to fish, we went about once every week or so to some place where they could throw in a line. Our favorite place was a little beach on Tampa

Bay under Gandy Bridge. There was enough beach for Kent and me to play and the fishing was good. Plus, the water was shallow and since it was the bay only little waves. We could swim, chase minnows, build sandcastles, all kinds of fun stuff while Mother and Daddy fished off the bridge. The beach was big enough that we would also sometimes camp there overnight. There was one night when we had set up camp on the beach, which is burned into my memory. Every year around the middle of August there is a major meteor shower. That is what we were hoping to see. Mother had made Kent and I both take naps that afternoon so we would be able to stay up late. We got to our little beach an hour or so before dark and got our camp all set up. Daddy started a fire just big enough to roast our hot dogs and a few marshmallows. Rather than keeping it going like we usually did when camping Daddy let the fire die out. We all lay in the sand and looked up at the stars. The night was clear, so the stars were really bright. I was starting to get sleepy when Kent cried, "There's one!" I saw it, too. A bright flash of light streaked across the night sky. I was wide awake after that and started looking for more. It didn't take long to see another, then another. Over the next two hours I saw dozens of these falling stars. Despite trying hard to stay awake, I soon drifted off. The sun was high in the sky when we all woke up the next day. We spent the morning on the beach, playing in the sand, fishing, and swimming in the shallows of the bay. All that day I thought of those falling stars. I couldn't help but wonder where they all had landed.

Since Mother, Daddy and Uncle Frank all liked to fish and we were living near the water, Daddy decided we needed a rowboat to go out into the bay. He soon found one that was cheap enough for us to afford. It needed a little work, but he and Uncle Frank got that little boat shipshape in their spare time. After that we went out into the bay to fish every week. I really liked riding in the boat even though I didn't fish. Kent was old enough he had a fishing pole, but I was still too little. I just played at one end of the boat with Pinkie while they fished. Some days Orangie and Dianne even came along out into the bay, too.

I liked it most days but there was one day that I didn't like one little bit. Everyone had been fishing for a couple hours and we were about to head back in when Mother got a bite on the line. Whatever it was, it put up quite a fight. I was watching intently when Mother pulled this big scary thing into the boat. It was flopping all over the bottom of the boat, headed straight for me. I decided I had no desire to stay in a boat with that scary thing, so I was headed overboard. I had almost made it over the side of the boat when Daddy managed to snag me by my underpants and pull me back in. By then Mother had the "scary thing" pinned down in the bottom of the boat. Once he was sure I wasn't going to jump ship again, Daddy got his foot on the "thing". While he held it down Mother carefully removed the hook from its mouth. Once it was off the line Daddy held it up so we could look it over. He said it was called a stingray. Now that Daddy had a good grip on it, I saw that it wasn't as scary as I first thought. I even got brave enough to touch it before we threw it back into the water. I must say it was soft and smooth. Not at all like the fish we usually caught.

That was not the last scary thing Mother caught but I was convinced by then jumping overboard was not the smartest thing I could do. I even stayed calm when Mother caught the hammerhead shark. Now talk about scary, that thing was downright ugly. We didn't throw that one back. Daddy took it to a man called a taxidermist and had it stuff so we could hang it on the wall when we finally got a house and settled down.

One of the nicest things about living in Tampa was the bananas. Every month or so Daddy would go to a place near us called Ybor City. There is a port there where the banana boats from South and Central America docked to unload their cargo. When they unloaded the boats, if there were any bananas that were too ripe to put in a truck to ship around the country, they threw them onto a big pile to sell there on the docks. Daddy could buy a whole big stalk of bananas almost as long as he was tall for less than a dollar. He would bring this home and tie it up in a tree near our trailer. He rigged it so that as we ate the bananas, he could lower it, that way we kids could always reach the bananas. The neighbor kids loved it. We could get a banana anytime we were hungry. Those bananas tasted better than any bananas I have ever eaten since.

As I said earlier, we often saw airplanes here. The trailer park was just past the end of the runway of MacDill Air Base. Several times a day one of the big DC-17 would take to the air and soar over us. One day when we were sitting on the swing set at the back of the park, one took off. Mother had come out with us and as we played, she stood and watched it climb skyward. As it disappeared, she called us over to her. She pointed to where it was just a tiny speck in the distance and asked us, "Did you see that plane as it took off?"

"We see them all the time," answered Kent. I just nodded.

"That is a special kind of airplane. It is a DC-17 also known as a Flying Fortress. Last year that airplane may have been one of the planes that helped break the Berlin Blockade. There is a city in Germany that is surrounded by Russian troops. The Russians wanted that city, so they blocked all the roads going into it. As a result, the only way the people who live there could get food to eat and coal to heat their houses was to have it flown in. The DC-17 took off every few minutes for almost a year bringing in what was needed. What do you think of that?"

"Wow!" we both said.

"And after a while one of the little girls in Berlin who used to wave at the pilots as then landed at Tempelhof Airport in Berlin, wrote a letter to the air force and asked if the pilots could please drop candy to them. And sure enough that is what they did. The pilots would make little parachutes with handkerchiefs and tie them to candy bars. That little girl's name was Mercedes."

Again, we both said WOW.

'Finally, the Russians gave up and allowed the trucks to drive the supplies in."

This is where we were living when Uncle Frank decided we needed a pet. Of course, he hadn't consulted Mother and Daddy about it. He just showed up with a box and in it was a baby alligator. He was a cute little thing. He was about a foot long when Uncle Frank brought him home. If he had stayed that size, he might have been an okay pet. But like all little animals, he grew. In a very short time, he was big enough to be a menace. We kids had learned very quickly, he was not a pet you could, well, pet. And when Daddy saw that he had begun to chew a hole in the box we kept him in, he decided he should put him in a bigger stronger box. To say that didn't go well is an understatement. As soon as Mother had cleaned and bandaged up the bite on Daddy's hand the alligator got to go to a new home in a swampy place out by where they had set up the bikes.

A few weeks after the alligator disaster, Uncle Frank brought another pet home for us. This time it was one we could actually play with and not risk losing a finger. It was a dog he had found wandering down a back road. It was black, had long hair, and was covered with dirt and fleas. He was also very skinny and afraid. Mother said we couldn't pet him or let him in the trailer until she had given him a good bath. So, Daddy tied him to a tree in the back of the lot until Mother could go to the store and get some Sunday Shower Flea Shampoo. That is a special dog shampoo that kills fleas and ticks as well as getting your dog clean. Before she left, she gave Daddy some scraps to feed our new dog and threatened us with unknown terrible things if we dared to go near the dog. So, Kent and I sat on the steps of the trailer and decided on what we were going to name him. In the meantime, Daddy filled the washtub from the hose at the bath house then put it in the sun to heat up a little bit. By that time, we had decided on a name. We were going to call him Blacky. Okay so we didn't pick the most original name, but it fit the dog to a tee.

As soon as Mother got back Daddy untied Blacky and put him in the tub. Mother poured Sunday Shower all down his back and started to rub it in. Man, were there a lot of fleas. By the time Mother was done, the top of the water was almost black with fleas floating there. Daddy emptied the tub in the palmettos while Mother hosed the shampoo off Blacky. Then she let us towel him dry. He was so fluffy, and he smelled great. Mother made him a bed out of an old blanket under the trailer. Then she found a chipped dish for his water dish. He was all settled in.

Years later when I was attending some training in Orlando, Mother joined me at the resort where it was held. It was a two-

week training course so over the weekend we drove off to the beach. On the way, as we drove toward the causeway we noticed the sign for MacDill Avenue. On a whim we turned and drove down it for a little way. Much to our surprise we found the trailer park. It had changed a lot. Instead of three rows of small trailers it was now one row of 60 feet long doublewides. But it was still there.

Kent and I on the seesaw in the trailer park in Tampa.

Playing under the awning in Tampa.

Cherie playing with her doll, Pinkie. If you look closely, you might spot Orangie and Diane.

Chapter Ten

Snakes! Storms!

As much as we liked it there in Tampa, we soon had to move on. This time we were moving north again toward the Panhandle of Florida. Remember me mentioning that snakes kept showing up in my life while here in Florida? Well, once again we encountered a snake. On the second day of this move we had stopped on the road for Daddy to take what I'll call a "natural break". The road was passing through a swampy area, and we had stopped just over a bridge across a small stream. When Daddy got out of the car, he had noticed a large cotton mouth moccasin down on the stream bank but since he didn't plan of leaving the roadbed, he thought nothing of it. Well, the moccasin had different ideas. This was his territory, and he wanted no intruders. Before Daddy got his business done and his pants zipped back up, that snake was coming up the bank toward him. Before he could get the car door opened and jump in, the snake was at his feet and preparing to strike. He ran to the other side of the car planning to jump in on that side, but the snake had gone under the car and had beaten him there. After a couple of back and forths like this, Daddy climbed on to the hood of the car. Seeing Daddy's odd behavior, Uncle Frank got out of the bus and yelled, "Hey Johnny, what's going on up there? Why are you up on the hood?"

Daddy called back to him, "There's a damn snake chasing back and forth under the car. It won't let me get in the car. Get the shotgun and kill this damn snake."

Uncle Frank carefully approached the car with the shot gun and sent the snake to reptile heaven. After Uncle Frank sent the snake to the snake's happy hunting ground, we got a good look at the aggressive booger. It was the first cottonmouth moccasin I'd seen up close and hoped it would be the last. After tossing it back into the stream bed we were on our way. One valuable lesson we learned from this was that cottonmouth moccasins are very aggressive snakes.

The next town we set up in was Port Richey. Our trailer was not parked in a very good place, so we didn't stay there all that long, but we were there long enough to experience a hurricane. Now talk about excitement! A few days before the storm hit, it was like the air was alive. It was hot and humid but very, very still. There was no wind at all. Everyone was busy getting things tied down and boarded up. Daddy and Uncle Frank had thrown big fat ropes over the trailer and tied them to a bunch of concrete blocks and great big spikes they had driven into the ground. When they had everything ready, Uncle Frank stayed with Kent and me while Daddy took Mother down to the beach to watch the big waves roll in. When they got back Mother had a surprise for us. She had a paper bag full of penny candy. She explained that we were going to have to be exceptionally good during the hurricane. Since she knew it would be hard to not be able to play outside, we could reach in the bag and get a treat three times a day. I was pretty excited about that and decided I was going to like this hurricane. Treats were right up there with some of my favorite things.

Shortly after that the storm started moving in. All went well for a while, until the trailer started rocking when gusts of wind hit it. Mother had the radio on so we could listen to the storm updates. Not long after the trailer started rocking, we heard an announcement advising everyone to take shelter. The radio listed all the evacuation shelters, and since one was near us Mother and Daddy decided that is where we should go. Next thing I knew Daddy was loading things into the car and Mother was collecting some of our toys, books, and her radio. She wanted to make sure we had everything we needed since we would be at the shelter until the storm was over. At least Mother, Kent and I would. Daddy and Uncle Frank were going to stay with the trailer during the storm. Daddy wrapped me up in a big old raincoat and carried me out to the car as Mother helped Kent struggle against the wind and rain. Even though we were between the trailer and the bus, the wind was blowing so hard we could hardly walk. I'm sure glad Daddy had a good hold on me, or I might have blown away. We went to a concrete block bakery a mile or so from where the trailer was parked. They had a big empty storage room where people were already gathering. Daddy spread my big green nap mat on the floor near the wall where there was an electrical outlet so Mother could plug in her radio. After they had unloaded the stuff, we had brought, Daddy kissed us all goodbye and headed back to the trailer. It was scary to think he and Uncle Frank were going to spend the night out there in this horrible storm.

It sure smelled good in this big building. Just like the fresh bread they were baking in a room off the storage room. Since we were the only ones with a radio, people drifted up from time to time to hear the latest news on the storm. The music and news on the radio were nice to have but I was especially happy to see that Mother had remembered to bring the treat bag. The first time I reached in, I got a licorice snail. Those were my favorites. I loved to unwind the little string of licorice chewing it up as I went. Then in the very center was a little bitty jaw breaker. If I ate it slowly enough, I could make it last almost an hour. You can see why it's my favorite.

We were there all night and part of the next day. But finally, the storm passed and we could go back to our trailer. Along the way we saw the damage the storm had caused. There were downed trees, parts of blown off roofs, and debris everywhere. Luckily, the trailer and bus had survived the storm with only minor damage. One of the ropes holding the trailer down had broken loose and the wind had ripped a screen off the bedroom window. The wind had blown something into the trailer and put a big dent in it but since it had so many other scrapes and dents it didn't matter. You hardly even noticed it. We were lucky that other than those minor things we were fine. Port Richey was a small town and Daddy and Uncle Frank

weren't doing much business, so we packed up once more and
moved on up the coast.

Chapter Eleven
Kent goes to School

From Port Richey we moved around the gulf coast to Pensacola at the end of the Florida Panhandle. By now Kent had had his sixth birthday and would soon be starting school. Daddy found a place for the bikes that was not only near a school for Kent, but we could park the trailer behind a gas station. The owner was a nice lady who let us run an extension cord to an outlet in the garage, so we had electricity. Mother had to carry water, but we could also use the restroom in the station which helped a lot. Mrs. Powell, the owner of the station, and Mother soon became good friends. This is where I made a new friend named Judy. In the back of the station was a pen where Mrs. Powell kept a tame raccoon. Kent and I would go visit Judy every day and take her little pieces of stuff to eat that we had saved from our lunch. We liked to watch her wash her food in the bowl of water in the corner of her cage before she ate it. Grapes were one of her favorites.

When fall came Kent entered first grade. His school was across the road and about a block down a dirt road. I never understand why Kent was afraid to walk to school by himself, but he sure was. So how did Mother solve this problem? Easy. I walked Kent to school each day. When we had finished breakfast and Kent was ready, hair neatly combed, face clean, and nice, clean shirt, even though it was the same one he had worn the last three days, I would take his hand and walk him to school. I, on the other hand, had managed to get my face and t-shirt dirty, before Mother could comb his hair and hand him his sack lunch. The T-shirt I had on would invariably show evidence of my breakfast and the training panties that finished off my outfit were dusty and baggy. We would head around the station and after we both looked both ways a few times, I led Kent across the street and down the road. I was careful on the way to school and didn't stop to play in any of the mud puddles since that might get Kent dirty. Once we reached his school, I'd say goodbye to him at the door to his classroom and head back home. I tried to stay out of the mud puddles and dust piles on the way back home and once in a while I even managed to do it, arriving home no dirtier than when I left. Okay, so I almost never managed to avoid the puddles and when I did it was usually because it hadn't rained and the puddles had dried up. I couldn't help it, it was just the way I was.

After I walked Kent to school, I had a whole day to play with Pinkie, Orangie and Dianne. Some days I'd go to the back lot where Daddy had the bikes and watch the boys ride the bikes around and around. Sometimes Daddy or Uncle Frank would take me a ride if I had been good and didn't "get into things."

When it was lunch time I'd walk to the trailer with Daddy and Uncle Frank. After lunch Mother would read me a story before I took my nap. Then when I woke up from my nap it would be time to go meet Kent and walk him home from school. Sometimes Mother would go with me to meet him but usually it was my job.

While we were in Pensacola, Uncle Frank kind of became famous. There was a day when one of the young men who hung out around the bikes stopped by on his way to go hunting. While they were "chewing the fat" a cardinal landed in the tree overhead. Before anyone could stop him, this guy pulled his rifle up and shot it. Boy, did Uncle Frank get mad! He grabbed the kid by the shoulders and shook him.

"Why did you do such a damned fool thing!" Uncle Frank yelled. "That's a songbird. Don't you know it's against the law to shoot songbirds? And besides, they don't harm anyone. They eat insects. Without them the world would be a foot deep in bugs!"

This crazy kid (that's what Uncle Frank called him when he told us about it later) called Uncle Frank bad names and stormed off. But that's not where the story ended. A couple days later That Crazy Kid showed up at our trailer as we were finishing up supper. He yelled for Uncle Frank to come outside; he had a present for him. When we all tumbled out of the trailer to see what he had brought, he grabbed a burlap bag out of the trunk of his car and emptied a big pile of dead songbirds at Uncle Frank's feet. I wanted to cry! There were dozens of beautiful colorful birds. Cardinals, bluebirds, orioles, and others I had never seen before. Oh, man, did Uncle Frank get mad then. He grabbed That Crazy Kid's gun and smashed the stock on the pavement. It shattered into about a million pieces. Then he went after That Crazy Kid. He hit him a couple good punches before Daddy pulled him off. That Crazy Kid jumped in his car and took off. As he was pulling away, he yelled out the window that he was getting the sheriff and Uncle Frank would be in big trouble then.

Once he left Daddy picked up the birds and put them back in the burlap bag. Uncle Frank headed into the gas station restroom to clean up and shave. I was really puzzled by that. Mother had a clean shirt for him when he came out of the restroom. When he had cleaned up and changed, we all sat down to wait.

Sure enough, That Crazy Kid showed up about an hour later and he had the sheriff with him. This was a sheriff we hadn't met yet, so Daddy, Uncle Frank and Mother all said hello politely and shook his hand. Kent and I had orders to stay in the trailer, but we watched through the window. Daddy did most of the talking. He started by showing the sheriff the dead birds. The sheriff pretty much just said so what. Then Daddy explained that shooting songbirds was against the law because they don't hurt anything and just eat bad bugs. The sheriff scratched his head and didn't seem to know what to think. In the end the sheriff took Uncle Frank in the car with him to go talk to the judge. Daddy picked up the bag of dead birds and followed them in our car. I don't know what happened when they saw the judge. I do know the outcome was Uncle Frank had a little vacation in the county jail and had to pay for That Crazy Kid's rifle. But That Crazy Kid had to pay a fine for every one of those birds he shot plus he had a vacation in jail, too. I heard Daddy telling Mother that what That Crazy Kid owed in fines was a lot more than what his rifle was worth. Also, his vacation was a lot longer than Uncle Frank's.

But that's still not the end of this story. A couple weeks later two ladies and a man drove up in a shiny new car. They were all dressed up in fancy clothes. The ladies had so much perfume on that I could smell them from where I stood by the trailer. The man was wearing a black suit and shiny shoes. He asked Mother if Mr. Frank Spencer was there. She said yes, he was at the back lot. Then she told me to run and get Uncle Frank and tell him he had company. I took off lickity split and ran to where Daddy and Uncle Frank were putting bikes together. When I told them some fancy people were at the trailer to see Uncle Frank, they picked up their grease rags and wiped their hand off. Daddy picked me up since no way I could keep up with two long legged Spencer men when they were in a hurry. When we got to the trailer Mother was chatting with the fancy people. Turning to us, she introduced them to Daddy and Uncle Frank. She said they were from some place called the Audubon Society. It turns out when Uncle Frank went on his vacation to jail there had been a report on him in the newspaper. These Audubon People had seen it and were there to give Uncle Frank a medal and a certificate. Once they gave him this stuff, they all shook his hand. They did that even though his hands were still greasy! Then they got in their shiny car and left. Mother and Daddy thought this was really something. All I could think was I couldn't wait to tell Kent about it. He was going to be really mad when he found out he had missed all the excitement.

All the time we had been in Florida, Kent and I had been fascinated with horny toads. They were ugly little lizards with bumps like little horns all over them. We were always trying to catch them and even managed to do that sometimes. When we did, we would put them in a cardboard box and pretend they were our pet dinosaurs. We would feed them dead flies and any other bug we could catch. Except spiders because Kent was really afraid of spiders. After a few days they would always get loose. Then we would go on a hunt for a new one.

Walking Kent to school

Kent as my plow horse.

Chapter Twelve
Back to Ohio

Kent had been in school for a couple of months when I could tell there was a problem brewing. Mother and Daddy did a lot of whispering. Another clue something was wrong was that Mother started talking a lot more about Ohio and all the family we had there. Then the next thing I knew Mother was packing suitcases for herself, Kent, and me. It turned out that Mother, Kent, and I were going to go on a long ride on a train to Ohio. I know I used to live there but I didn't remember it at all. Daddy was going to stay here because he didn't want to go back to Ohio. He wanted to stay here with Uncle Franks and the bikes. I wasn't sure if we were going to come back or if Daddy was going to come join us later in Ohio. It was kind of a scary time, not knowing for sure what was going to happen. I liked the way we were living but I knew Mother and Kent didn't like it all that much. Mother was worried about Kent's schooling if we kept moving around like this. Kent seemed to have trouble finding friends each time we moved. I, on the other hand, always had friends. Orangie and Dianne were always there.

Later that week a special letter came in the mail from my grandfather, and we were all ready to go. Mother explained that Grandpa worked for the railroad so he could get our tickets cheaply. Blacky was going to go with us. Daddy had bought a cage big enough for Blacky to ride in comfortably. Mother said he would have to ride in the baggage car with our big suitcases, but he would be just fine. She would put his blanket in it for him to sleep on. She would give the baggage handler some food for him and put in his water dish.

So, a few days later, our bags were packed. We had our tickets. We were ready to go. The next afternoon Daddy drove us with all our suitcases and Blacky in his cage to the train station.

When we got there, I didn't know whether to be excited or scared. Daddy helped us get everything to the platform where we had to wait for the train. Kent and I sat quietly on a bench back from the tracks and I was so glad we were not out standing near the tracks when the train came in. We could see the engine coming from a long way down the track. When it pulled in, the wheels screamed and threw off sparks as it came to a stop. It was huge! The wheels were taller than I was. As soon as it had fully stopped, Daddy gave most of our bags to the porter who loaded them into the baggage car. After we all kissed Daddy goodbye, Mother, Kent, and I climbed up the ladder like steps into the train. We found our seats and there on the other side of the window was Daddy waving goodbye some more. We had just gotten settled when the train started to move. I watched until I could no longer see Daddy standing on the platform waving goodbye. I tried not to cry but tears trickled down my cheeks anyway. I didn't know when I would see him again.

We were on the train for a long time. Shortly after we waved goodbye to Daddy it got dark, and Kent and I curled up in the seat and went to sleep. Sometime during the night, as we were passing through Birmingham, Mother woke us up to see a big statue. She said it was a statue of someone named Vulcan. He had a spear in his hand that was pointing toward the sky and was glowing green. I watched it until it was out of sight then I went back to sleep again.

The next morning our train was traveling through hills. Everything was green but soon some other colors started showing in the trees. After all it was almost my birthday, so it was now fall. I would be turning four this year. Almost a big girl.

The next day, just before we stopped at a town, Mother had been talking to the porter about food. She had thought she would buy food on the train but had no idea it would be so expensive. She had brought some sandwiches with us, but they were long gone. We still had a couple more days on the train, so we had to eat. The porter- he is the man who helps you with things on the train- told Mother at the next stop she should have time to get to a place that sold sandwiches and back to the train. It was a long stop since they had to load mail and other cargo there. He gave her directions. She told us to behave and stay in our seats. As soon as the train stopped, she climbed down the steps and headed out to find the shop. It seemed like she had been gone forever. The porter kept checking on us and to see if she was back yet. He would smile and tell us she would be here any minute, but I could tell he was beginning to get worried. By this time Kent and I were getting worried, too. What would happen to us if she didn't get back before the train left? We sat with our noses to the window watching the entrance to the street she had gone down. The conductor started blowing his whistle for the train to move on when I spotted her running up the street toward the station. She had almost reached the train when it started to move. Kent and I were crying by now because we were sure she would not make it. The porter was hanging out the door of our train car encouraging her to hurry. She got to the door before the train picked up speed and the porter managed to grab Mother and pull her on board just in time.

"That was a close one, Young Lady," the porter said as Mother caught her breath. "You almost didn't make it."

"I'm so sorry," she replied. "It looked like half the train had the same idea. Thank you so much for helping me."

Mother hugged us both when she joined us. It was still a long way to go but at least we had food and Mother had made it before the train left.

As the train sped through the countryside toward Ohio, Mother entertained us by reading from our big book, "Song of the South" and talking about all the relatives we would be meeting soon. The first relative would be our grandpa. He would meet us at the station when we got to Columbus. She told us all about him. He was a big man with white hair. He was very smart. He bought the tickets for us so he must be kind too. Humm. Now that sounds very familiar. Then it hit me. My Grandpa must be Uncle Remus. How great is that? I bet he could tell good stories, too. I was so excited I almost peed my pants. My Grandpa was Uncle Remus! I could hardly wait to get to Columbus.

It was late in the afternoon when the train finally pulled into Union Station in Columbus. We helped Mother gather our belongings and checked under the seat to make sure we hadn't forgotten anything. We bid goodbye to the nice porter and thanked him for all his help. He waved to us after he handed down our carry-on bag. Then we turned away and started looking for Grandpa.

"There he is," Mother cried. "Pop! Over here!"

I noticed she was waving to a white-haired man who was hurrying our way. But there had to be a mistake. That was not Uncle Remus. This man had white hair alright, but he also had white skin. Not the brown skin that Uncle Remus had. It was all wrong. But here was Mother smiling ear to ear and hugging this man. Kent was grinning and shaking his hand.

But you weren't fooling me. No way. This was not my grandfather. My grandfather was Uncle Remus.

The next thing I knew he was loading our luggage in the trunk of his car and Mother and Kent were piling in. What choice did I have? I had to stay with Mother. I decided she would finally figure it out and we would go find my real Grandpa.

Well, it turns out I had it all wrong. Uncle Remus was just in the book and not real. And this man was really my grandpa. It took me a while, but I finally came around. The next few days were a whirlwind of meeting relatives and in the end, we landed at Yantie's house in Laurelville. I learned then that the reason we had come back to Ohio was because Yantie's husband, Uncle Bill, was very sick and she needed Mother's help to take care of him. Mother, Kent, and I moved into one of the big upstairs bedrooms. I missed Daddy but other than that I liked living here.

We had only been there a couple weeks when Uncle Bill passed away. I kept expecting Mother to tell us we would be going back to Florida, but she seemed to be content to stay here. Maybe because Kent had started school.

Kent had started school as soon as we got there but this time he decided to walk to school alone. The school was only three houses from Yantie's, so he didn't have to go far. There were no streets to cross so it was easy peasy. And I must say I was very glad he didn't need me. One of the things Mother forgot to tell me about Ohio was it is really cold here.

Shortly after we got to Laurelville, I had my birthday. It was pretty cool. Not only did I get presents and a cake but the next night I got to dress up in funny clothes and go around all over town and people gave me candy and treats. Okay, not just me. All the kids got candy, too. It is a thing called Trick or Treat and the best thing about it is they do it every year.

I was almost done with my Trick or Treat candy when the next big day approached- Thanksgiving. We had had a little bigger meal than usual on this day when we were in Florida but from the talk, I was hearing this was going to be a huge meal. Mother and Yantie talked about the food they would prepare as they did the housework. I listened closely so I could report to Kent on what we were going to have when he got home from school. So far as I could tell, the menu consisted of turkey, dressing, gravy, yams, green beans, cranberry salad, pickles, beets, and pies! Lots of pies! Yantie made the best pies. She made pies every couple of days, and she always made one little pie especially for me. It was my favorite. She called it a sugar pie and said it was sweet like me. I'm not sure about that but I really liked that pie. To make it she used the leftover bits of crust from the other pies and after rolling it out put it in a little pie tin. She said it was just my size. Then she put two handfuls of flour into the crust in the pie tin. To that she added a handful of sugar and a little cinnamon. Next, she poured in some milk and stirred it with her figure until it felt right. The last step is to dot it with butter and pop it in the oven. I could hardly wait for it to come out. There was a custardy layer on the bottom and a milk layer on the top. Yum!

The day before Thanksgiving, Mother and Yantie were cooking all day. In the afternoon Grandma and Grandpa with my Uncle Ned arrived. By bedtime all but the turkey and the last-minute dishes were done. My belly growled all night from smelling all those good smells.

Thanksgiving Day dawned clear and cold. As soon as we were dressed, Kent and I were shooed out of the house. We had just decided what to play when Yantie stuck her head out the door and handed Kent a basket. We were ordered to go up to the barn and gather the eggs. We sprinted past the out-building up the driveway to the barn. By the time we got there our cheeks were rosy from the cold. It was warmer in the barn and smelled of chickens. At the far end of the barn was the chicken coop. We walked past the well pump and carefully opened the door and went in with the chickens. Kent closed the latch on the door then we began checking each nest, looking to see if a hen had left an egg there for us. By the time we had all the nests checked, we had a full basket of warm fresh eggs. The chickens were clucking peacefully as we let ourselves out of the coop. Before we left Kent checked the water and food dishes, but they were both full. Mr. Ingles must have been up to feed them but forgot to gather the eggs. (I'll tell you more about Mr. Ingles later.)

When we stepped out of the barn we were greeted by a cold wind. The sky had clouded over, too. Being careful not to drop the eggs, we hurried back to the house. When we got there the kitchen was warm from all the cooking that had been going on. We gave Yantie the eggs then went up to our room to stay out of the way. Our time outside had made the cozy bedroom feel good.

By the middle of the afternoon dinner was ready. And what a meal. I've never seen so much food. We ate and ate and ate. Later in the afternoon, Uncle Dot and Aunt Dorie stopped by for a short visit. They lived on a big dairy farm just north of town. I loved going up to their house. It was huge. It was made of stone and had a big porch on the front. One day when I was there visiting Aunt Dorie with Yantie. While we were there, Aunt Dorie asked me to come with her, she had something to show me. She took my hand and led me toward the big barn. Once there we climbed the ladder up to the haymow. When we came out in the big room over the milking chamber I was met with a big pile of brightly colored sacks.

"Uncle Dot gets his feed in these pretty sacks. Now I want you to tell me which ones you want me to save for you so we can make you some nice sun dress for next summer," Aunt Dorie told me.

I was overwhelmed. So many pretty colors. Finally, I settled on two purple flowered sacks and a bright pink one.

I wandered over and crawled up on Uncle Dot's lap. I listened to the conversation, but it was mostly about people and things I didn't know anything about. Just before they started to get ready to leave, Uncle Dot asked Grandpa, "Cloyce, are you planning on going home tonight?"

"Well, I hadn't planned on it. I was thinking of leaving tomorrow morning," replied Grandpa.

"You might want to rethink that. The weather report I heard just before we came down was calling for snow tomorrow. They made it sound like it was going to be a good amount."

They talked about the pros and cons and leaving today and finally Grandpa decided they should go. He had animals to feed anyway. He didn't want to get stuck here if it was a good amount of snow. Turns out it was a good thing he decided to go home. Not only did we get snow, but we also got a full-blown blizzard.

I woke the next morning to an eerie quiet. I rose up from my bed on the floor and looked out the window. All I could see was white. It was so cold outside, the cold was seeping through the windowpane. Ice crystals had even begun to form along the edges of the windowpane. Lacy fingers of ice reaching out toward the center of each pane. Mother had laid out my clothes and I dressed as quickly as possible. Then I headed downstairs to the kitchen where it would be warmer. I was not surprised to see that everyone was gathered there. I could hear Mr. Ingles in the basement stoking the furnace. The furnace was under the kitchen and the shovel made scraping sounds as he shoveled up the coal. That was followed by the clang as the shovel hit the side of the furnace door. Finally, there was a bang as he closed the door. In a few minutes he appeared at the basement door. He headed to the washroom off the kitchen to wash the coal dust off his hands before joining us at the table.

"Well, what do you think of the snow, Petty?" Yantie asked me. She called everyone Petty. I never figured out why, but I guess that was just Yantie.

"I'm not sure. It just looks all white," I replied.

"It sure is," she laughed as she dished up some cornmeal mush.

I started to eat and Yantie handed a bowl to Mr. Ingles. He was a left over from the Tourist Home Yantie and Uncle Bill had run before Uncle Bill got sick. Back before motels people who were traveling stopped at Tourist Homes. They were like regular houses, but you could rent a room for a night or more, Usually, it was just for a short time. Mr. Ingles was different. He had come intending to do some real estate deals in the area but never moved on. It might have been because Yantie was such a good cook. After a few years he was like family. He helped with the chores when needed, like stoking the furnace.

The snow continued coming down all that day and when we went to bed it still hadn't let up. The wind howled and the temperature dropped. Through the night Mother and Mr. Ingles took turns stoking the furnace. The next day I woke to more snow falling. It wasn't until late the second day that the snow finally let up. It was still falling a little, but I could at last see what it looked like outside. The snow had been so thick for the last two days that I couldn't see anything but a sheet of white. That's when I remembered the chickens. Turning to Yantie, I cried, "The chickens! They haven't been feed and watered! They must be really hungry and thirsty. We have to go feed them."

Mother snagged me as I was struggling into my coat on my way to the door. "Slow down," she said, "There is no way you can get to the barn through this snow. Tomorrow we will try to get a path cleared and then we can worry about the chickens. Until then they will be just fine."

All that night I worried about the hungry chickens. I was sure I could have gotten to them if Mother would only have let me. After all the snow looked nice and flat. I could have just walked on top of it. That shows you how much I knew about snow. You need to remember this was the first snow I could remember ever seeing. I wondered if it had snowed in Florida where Daddy was.

The next morning when I came downstairs to breakfast the sun was shining and I got a good look at the snow. Mr.

Ingles had started clearing a path to the barn. Mother said that as soon as we ate, Kent and I could go out and play in it. I could hardly wait. I had never seen snow before, and it looked soft and fluffy. Boy was I in for a shock.

I became more and more impatient as Mother started dressing me to go out. I was surprised that Mother told me to leave my warm flannel pjs on. Then she put a sweater over them. Last of all she put me into what she called a snow suit. It was this puffy one-piece thing that covered me head to toe. Ok, almost head to toe. It ended at my ankles but from there it went all the way up with a hood that covered my head. The only thing not covered were my feet, my hands, and my face. Once she poured me into it, she zipped the zipper that ran up one leg all the way across my belly and to my neck. Before she let me stand up, she put on my shoes and pushed some rubber shoe-things she called goulashes on over my shoes and buckled them around my ankles Last step was to put mittens on my hands. I tried to stand up but could hardly move.

"I'm going to cook in this! I'm so hot I can hardly breath," I complained.

"You will be fine when you get outside," she assured me.

Kent had managed to don his snow gear by himself as I was being prepared for my first adventure in the snow. I waddled behind him to the back door and out we went. I gasped when the cold air hit my face. I had never been where it was this cold before. What we called cold days in Florida I only needed a heavy sweater. I quickly changed my mind about the need for a snow suit.

Kent had run ahead of me on the path leading to the barn. I waddled uncertainly behind him to explore this new wonder- snow. Lesson number one- snow was slippery. I took a step off the back step and headed out. Two steps later I was on my butt in the middle of the path. My feet had shot out from under me and down I went. Lesson number two- snowsuits make it hard to maneuver. I finally struggled to my feet and started out again. Once I was upright, I carefully took a step forward. All the time Kent was yelling for me to hurry up.

I soon got my snow legs so to speak and ventured forward to join Kent. The snow on either side of the path was so deep I had to stand on tip toes just to see over the top. Getting brave I grabbed a hand full and held it up to my face since that was the only part of my body that was exposed. Lesson number three- snow is very cold and wet.

When I finally made it to the barn it surprised me how warm it felt when I walked in the door. Kent had already gathered the eggs and Mr. Ingles had finished feeding the chickens, so we turned around and headed back toward the house. By the time we got there I was getting cold even with all the clothes I had on. When we tumbled in the door Mother made us stand on a rug and peel off our wet clothes. Once we were down to our pjs she sent us upstairs to get dressed. As we headed up to our bedroom, she hung our snowsuits in the basement stairwell to dry.

We spent the day listening to stories on Mother's record player and playing with our toys until lunch time. From time to time, we looked out the window to check how much of the road and sidewalk had been cleared. From the window we could see all the way to the center of town. The snowplows and men with shovels had been making progress on clearing paths and a road just wide enough for one car to slip past another on the street in front of the house.

We spent the rest of the first day after the snow stopped inside. It was still very cold, and a wind was blowing the snow into drifts. The second day was a little warmer and the wind had died. After we ate breakfast, Mother asked if we would like to walk downtown with her to see some more of the snow. Once we got our snow gear pulled on over our clothes, we went out the front door. Mr. Ingles had cleared a path to the road and broken a way through the mountain of snow the plows had piled up, so we could walk in the road. Since there were no cars to speak of this was the only way to get around.

When we got to the center of town, we found a huge pile of snow in front of the hardware store. It looked like a mountain. It was too tempting to pass up, so Kent and I began climbing it. It took a while but when we reached the top, we could see the roof of the hardware store. Then it hit me. Getting up had been a struggle but how was I supposed to get down? I stood there puzzling about it for a while. Kent, of course, figured it out right way. He sat down and pushed off. I watched as he slid down the side of the snow pile. It looked like fun, so I was right behind him.

The piles of snow lasted for weeks. It was still on the ground for Christmas. The mountains of snow along the roads would last even longer. I was hoping Daddy would come for Christmas or we could go back to Florida but that didn't happen. I wasn't sure why we were still here. Uncle Bill, Yantie's husband, had passed away shortly after we got to Ohio, so Mother was no longer needed. I mean, I thought we had come to Ohio to take care of him. But it seemed that Mother was not in a hurry to go back to our gypsy life. She kept pointing out Kent was in school so needed to stay in one place.

When winter started to give way to spring and we were waiting for Daddy to join us or for us to go back to Florida, we started getting presents from Daddy in the mail. We were puzzled when the first one came. Why would Daddy send us a soup can? He had put a piece of paper around it with our names and address where the label should be, and the can lid was spot welded back on. When we pried the lid off, a horny toad poked his head out. We were so excited. We hadn't found any of them here in Ohio, so this was a real treat. We found a big cardboard box for its home and began hunting for flies to feed it. Mother suggested it might like some of the trimmings from the vegetables in the kitchen. She even found an old window screen to put over the box so it wouldn't get out. Those weeks when we were waiting, Daddy sent us several more. Soon we had a regular zoo in our cardboard box.

The only problem with our zoo was Yantie did not like it one little bit. Mother had to reassure her constantly that they were harmless and wouldn't escape. She was doubtful. Anything that looked like they did, had to be dangerous. Then came the weekend near Easter when we went to visit Grandma and Grandpa. They lived a couple hours' drive from us and with the weeks of bad weather we couldn't just go anytime. We hadn't seen them since Thanksgiving. I had slowly come to understand that Uncle Remus was not a real person so he couldn't be my grandpa, but it was still a little disappointing. We had a good visit. Grandma gave us all kinds of things we usually didn't get. Like Pepsi. My Uncle Ned liked it, so they kept it all the time. Uncle Ned was a special person. He had the body of a man, but he was still a child like me. Mother explained that he had been born this way. He had lots of toy trucks and he let Kent and I play with them. It was hard to understand him at first but once I learned his language we got along just fine.

When we got back to Yantie's we found a terrible thing had happened. She had moved our zoo up to the barn as soon as we left, and all our horny toads had escaped. We searched high and low for them, but they could not be found. After a few days we gave up.

I need to add a follow up story here. We did eventually find one of the horny toads the following summer. It was a prefect warm summer day. We were playing with the neighbor kids at the school grounds up the street from our house. Suddenly we heard Mr. Durant making a fuss. He was a sweet old man who lived beside the school. He was in his garden and going after something with his hoe. We all made a bee line over to see what had him so upset. When we got there to our horror it was one of our horny toads that he was hacking at. The poor little beast was spritely hopping back and forth trying to avoid his hoe. We all started pleading with him to stop! Telling him it was our pet. He kept yelling to stay back it was poisonous. Sadly, we were not successful in convincing him it was harmless until too late. Since he felt so bad (I told you he was a sweet man) he gave us an empty cigar box to scoop up the remains. We carried it home humming a funeral dirge to bury it in the back year under the cherry tree. The funeral was a success with hymns, prayers, and a sermon. And, of course, mourners providing ample tears.

Spring came and the mountain of snow in the center of town finally melted. The grown-ups talked a lot about when and if Daddy was coming to get us when they didn't know I was listening. I think Yantie kind of hoped he wouldn't come back. I didn't share this with Kent, but I was really worried. Then one night just before we were going to sleep, we heard a familiar voice singing as footsteps sounded on the stairs. "If you're in Arizona I'll follow you. If you're in Minnesota, I'll be there, too." Mother jumped off the bed and started for the door just as Daddy opened it and walked in. He was home.

Kent in front of the snow in downtown Laurelville

Kent and Cherie in the back yard.

Chapter Thirteen
Last Hurrah

Our gypsy days were almost over. Daddy and Uncle Frank did try a couple more times to make a go of it with the bikes. But for the most part we stayed in Laurelville at Yantie's. At the beginning of summer, they set up in a small town in Michigan called Benton Harbor. Once they were settled and Daddy had a trailer set up for us, we joined him. Mother packed the car full. I mean really full. There was room on the front seat for her and Kent. I sat in the front seat part of the time until Kent complained he was crowded. That was my cue to crawl up in the tunnel Mother had made between the stuff stacked to the ceiling of the car so she could see out the back window. It was a cozy place and I usually fell asleep. The trip was a long one. We left before the sun was up and drove all day and into the night. I was asleep when we got there and don't remember how I got into the trailer and put to bed. When I woke up the next day, I was in my new home.

We were set up in a large lot behind a gas station run by a family named King. They turned out to be our good friends while we were there. They had a son my age called Richard and we were soon best buddies. I had a speech problem at that age making it hard to say many things. When I said his name, it came out Ritree rather than Richie. The S sound was a stranger to me, and the Th and F sounds and I only had a passing acquaintance. He seemed to be the only one who understood me, so we got along just fine.

Michigan was as the book says, "the best of times and the worst of times." In the best category they had a place called The House of David. It was a park run by a religious group of men who had long beards. It was part garden and part zoo. Adults could go in for just a quarter and kids were free. Mother would take Kent and I there with a sack lunch and we could spend hours. There was a restaurant, but we didn't have the money to eat there so we had a picnic instead. The very best part of the park was the train. We could ride a small train all around the park, past the unusual plants and exotic animals in cages. It was the best!

The other best was when the circus came to town. Mother took us to the tracks where the circus train was unloading. We didn't stay there very long though because we needed to stake out our spot for the parade. And what a parade! There were elephants, lions in cages, fire-eaters, jugglers. bareback riders and so much more. I was so excited I couldn't wait to go to the circus and see it all.

Then the bad new hit. Mother found out how much the tickets cost. They were way more than our budget. But again, good news stepped in and saved the day. At least a little bit. At the local movie theater "The Greatest Show on Earth" was playing so we got to go there instead. It was not the same but was almost as good and Kent and I got in for free.

Now for the worst of times. This was the early 1950's when everyone was sure that we were going to be attacked from the air. The Korean War was going on somewhere far away, but the radio and newspapers were full of warnings. As a result, the local mothers were doing their part to prepare us for the inevitable. That plane that would fly over and drop a big bomb on top of us. It became a regular part of our day to be playing in the big empty field behind the bike track and to hear one of the women in the neighborhood yell, "Hit the dirt!" Every kid as far as you could see would drop to the ground and cover their heads with their arms as best they could. As an adult I realized how foolish this was. If a bomb had been dropped, and they were thinking atomic bombs at this point, covering our heads would not have done much to save us. We were never sure if this was just a game or something terrifying. I went back and forth with it for months. Even after we were no longer hitting the dirt I would listen in fear if I heard an airplane go over at night. I would strain to hear that whistling sound of the bomb falling through the air to blast me to smithereens.

There were also some personal worsts here. I went through either a clumsy or unlucky time. It started when Ritree and I were digging a hole to China. I mean, everyone knows if you dig far enough you will come out on the other side of the world. And what is there? China. Ritree had an old rusty shovel he would loosen the dirt with and then I would scoop it out. We were working as a well-oiled machine when the gears shifted. I scooped as he was digging and my head sort of got in the way. The result was a nice sized gash on the top of my head, and we all know how head wounds bleed. End result- I had a bad headache and a scab on my head. Also, we never got to China.

Then a few days later, we were all wandering around at the very back of the field near the woods picking the late summer wildflowers when I discovered a ground bumble bee's nest. By "discovered" I mean stepped right in it. They nailed me but good. Kids scattered every which way. I ran for home and as luck would have it as I ran screaming by a neighbor's garden, he had the hose out watering. It didn't take him long to figure out I needed to be sprayed down. I arrived back at the trailer, dripping wet and the proud owner of a dozen or so bee stings. Mother dabbed baking soda on them and put me in dry clothes. Her nursing skills came in handy as usual.

The last of my worst of times was my own silly fault. I am ashamed to admit I had a habit of throwing temper tantrums. Since speech was not my strong suit Kent could out argue me every time. I would start talking, trying to say what was on my mind, but it would be so garbled he would start laughing which made me even more frustrated. Finally, I would solve the problem by throwing myself down on the ground and kicking and screaming. He, of course, found it quite amusing. On the afternoon of my worst event, Kent and

Ritree and I were playing Tarzan under the trees behind the trailer where Daddy had a couple of bikes parked. Mother had given us some old silverware to use as our knives to fight off the lions, and gorillas, and boa constrictors. The problem arose when I was given a butter knife not a regular table knife. I wanted a knife like the boys had. I didn't care if this was the kind of knife Jane liked the best. It wasn't fair. I wanted… At that point, my frustration kicked in. I hit the dirt so to speak. Unfortunately, the dirt I hit was already occupied by a bike. My head hit the kickstand. Blood poured forth. I didn't want to play any stupid Tarzan game anymore anyway. Mother put a butterfly bandage on it, but I probably needed a stitch or two. To this day, I still have a scar on my forehead.

We were still there when school started that fall. Kent would be starting second grade, and I was sure I would be starting Kindergarten. After all, Ritree was five and I was going to be five at the end of October. So surely, I could go to school, too. Mother was praying I could go to school, I am sure. I think she was at the point where she needed a break. So, we all walked the block or so over to the school to get us enrolled. I had on a clean dress and for once managed to keep it clean until I got there. I was so thrilled when I saw the amazing playground. Swings, slides, a giant stride, and the biggest, most awesome jungle gym you had ever seen. I couldn't wait to spend my days playing on all that super equipment.

Then we went inside. Kent got enrolled. Ritree got enrolled. Then it was my turn.

"And Cheryl's birthday is when?" asked the nice lady writing everything down.

"October 30th. She will be five," said Mother sweetly.

"Oh, dear," said the lady smiling sadly. "I'm afraid she is too young. The cutoff date is September 30th."

What? Am I hearing right? I can't go to school! As it sunk in the tears started to flow. "But Ritree gets to go to school," I said in my most pathetic voice. And if there was one thing, I was good at it was pathetic. "If he gets to go, why can't I?"

The nice lady started to patiently explain. The tears continued to flow. The sobs started. Mother looked crestfallen. Kent looked embarrassed. The nice lady looked bewildered. About this time a man in a pinstriped suit walked over.

"What seems to be the issue here?" he asked.

The nice lady explained. Mother looked pleading. I looked pathetic. Long story short- they let me in. I got to go to school. Of course, it was not exactly as I thought it would be. They had some silly rules. You couldn't get up and go talk to Ritree whenever you wanted. You only got to play on the playground a short time each day. And lots of other rules but all in all I liked it. So, I was sad when after a month and a half, Daddy announced that they were packing up the bikes and heading back to Ohio. The weather was turning cold, and the business had dropped off to the point he wasn't making any money. So Yantie's house here we come.

We packed it all up and headed south. Back in Ohio, Daddy bought a nice big trailer that we put in Yantie's back yard. Kent got enrolled in school there. I discovered Laurelville didn't have Kindergarten, so I was at home again. Our gypsy days were over for good. Daddy found a job that brought home a regular paycheck. Mother helped out at the local doctor's office. I hung out with Yantie while Mother was gone. Life fell into a pattern. One that was more of a normal pattern than the one I had lived for the last few years. But I guess somewhere in my psyche I will also be that little towheaded servicycle gypsy.